FIGHTER'S MERCY

A. RIVERS

Cover design by Steamy Designs

Sensitivity editing by A Book A Day Author Services

Editing by Paper Poppy Editorial

Proofreading by Hot Tree Editing

Prologue

I lie on a hotel bed with a sleeping stranger, and my body feels wrung out in the best possible way. Three times he made me fall apart. *Three*. Without even exchanging names. My ex-boyfriend sometimes couldn't get me there once, and it had been a long while since he bothered trying.

I study the arm of the man I've dubbed Mr. Tattoos. The red roses that bloom on his shoulder and wind around his bicep should look feminine, but something about the way they're interspersed with black and gray means they aren't. They're sexy. Beautifully masculine. A perfect match for the confident lover I lured away from the bar tonight.

His arm flexes in his sleep, and I freeze, hoping he'll remain dead to the world. He murmurs drowsily, curves his hand around my hip, and settles again. He's lying on his front with his face turned toward me. Even his bone structure is a work of art. High cheekbones, a perfectly straight nose, and a defined jaw. When I think of the way he handled me—gently, but not as though I'm fragile—it makes me reluctant to leave. Something drew me to this

1

man. I thought having sex with him a couple of times would be enough, but I yearn to snuggle into his hard body and be close to him.

That is not okay.

This is supposed to be a meaningless one-night stand to help me move on from Chad. The last thing I need is to become intrigued by Mr. Tattoos's soulful blue eyes or the inky eyelashes that cast shadows over his cheeks in the moonlight. I'm barely holding it together after my last relationship. I don't have the emotional bandwidth for anything new.

I edge away from him, holding my breath as his arm flops from my hip onto the bed, but he doesn't show any sign of waking. I place one foot on the carpet, then the other, and ease off the mattress so I can search for my clothes on the floor. I find my dress and pull it over my head, then feel around until my hand closes over my purse. I don't bother with my underwear or bra. It's more important to get out of here without disturbing him. I've never slept with a stranger before, which means I haven't had to do an awkward morning after, and I'd rather not begin now.

I tiptoe across the room, collect my shoes from near the door, and grab the handle. He still hasn't stirred. I crack the door open, then pull it wider until I can slip through the gap. When it closes behind me, I let out a sigh of relief but don't wait around in case the click of the latch snaps him out of his dream. I take off along the corridor. My first walk of shame is more of a run.

That should have been the end of it. But in reality, that night was only the beginning.

ONE

6 Months Later

MERCY

I roll my suitcase across the asphalt driveway toward a building that looks like it came straight from the Italian countryside. Pale orange walls, a reddish roof, and behind it are grapevines as far as the eye can see. It's idyllic. The perfect setting for my best friend Isiah's wedding. And hopefully a good place for me to forget about the growing stack of unpaid bills on the counter at home. I cringe at the thought of the letter that arrived this morning, reminding me of the costs owing for Danny's funeral. Insult to injury, considering the medical bills related to trying to keep him alive are what got me into financial trouble in the first place. But I'll pay. Somehow. Meanwhile, during my time in Napa Valley, I intend to do my best to forget.

I check in at the front counter and the receptionist hands me a set of keys. Isiah booked accommodation for the entire bridal party in the lead-up to the wedding. I'm halfway along the corridor when I hear a voice that stops me in my tracks. I strain my ears, trying to hear it again.

"...so glad there's air conditioning," the disembodied female voice continues. "It's hot out there."

My jaw drops.

It can't be.

But I swear the woman sounds just like my Miss Mystery—who gave me the most incredible night of my life and then vanished. I'd hoped our hours together might lead to something more. She'd been gorgeous, with just a hint of vulnerability that intrigued me. She'd said one night only, but I thought I'd have the chance to talk her around. Except she left before dawn. Out of respect for her wishes, I didn't try to find her. But now, it seems, the universe has handed me a golden opportunity.

I follow the sound of voices—someone else is speaking now—around a corner and into a small communal area where a pair of sofas face each other. On the far side, Hazel, Isiah's bride-to-be, is seated beside a pale brunette, her best friend. Seated opposite, with her back to me, is a woman in a black tank top, with an elegantly sloped neck and toned shoulders. A memory flashes into my mind of me lowering my mouth to the curve of her neck and sucking on her rich, brown skin until she shivered.

"Hey, Mercy." Hazel gets to her feet and comes around to hug me. I smile but I can't take my eyes off her companion. "Did you have a good trip?"

"It was a nice drive," I reply on autopilot. Miss Mystery is starting to turn, but I can't tell if she recognizes me.

"I think you've met my maid of honor, Karen," Hazel says.

The brunette waggles her fingers in a flirty wave. I nod to her.

"And this is my childhood best friend, Tempe. She's the bridesmaid."

Tempe.

I finally have a name to go with the face and body that have been haunting my dreams.

Tempe's deep brown eyes lock on mine and she stiffens. Oh yeah, she recognizes me.

"You," she breathes. "Oh my God."

That's when she stands up and I see what I couldn't before.

She's pregnant.

Her belly is rounded enough that there's no doubting it. The air seizes in my lungs. Based on the size of the bump, she's five or six months along, which means she either moved on from me quickly or was already pregnant when we were together. Neither option is something I want to dwell on.

"Congratulations." I force myself to smile. "You look great."

Her jaw firms and she rounds the sofa and grabs my arm. "Excuse me," she says to her friends. "We'll be back soon."

She tugs me away from them. I barely have the presence of mind to drag my suitcase behind us. I follow her around several corners, not processing where we're going. My mind is too busy protesting the unfairness of finally seeing her again when I apparently won't have a chance to pursue anything with her. She stops in a small alcove beside the ladies' room. I find myself scanning her fingers for a ring, but don't see one.

"Here's the thing." Her words are choked, and I get the feeling she's barely holding herself together, although I'm not sure why. She's clearly moved on, so what would make her so upset about running into an old fling? Sure, it's awkward under the circumstances, but it's hardly enough to warrant the expression of dread that's twisting her features. "Shit, this is hard."

"What is it?" I ask, hoping I sound encouraging. If

5

she's trying to gently let me know we won't be having a repeat, I kinda figured as much the second I laid eyes on her baby bump.

She clears her throat and looks me straight in the eye. "You're the father of my baby."

————

TEMPE

"What?"

I curse myself as I watch the color leach from Mr. Tattoos's perfectly sculpted face. His lips part and a breath of air passes between them. I'm not sure there's a right way to tell someone they're about to become a dad, but I think I did it wrong.

I touch his upper arm. "Are you okay?"

I try to remember what Hazel called him but come up empty. I hadn't been paying much attention at that point. I'd been more distracted by how inconvenient it was to get hot flashes during summer in California. It's scorching enough without hormones getting in on the action.

"Hey." I grip his arm a bit more firmly. Is he going into shock or something?

"I'm okay," he says. "I just…" He trails off. "My brain is still catching up. Give me a second."

My mouth quirks. He hasn't flipped his lid yet, which is positive, although based on his reaction, yep, I definitely need to work on my delivery skills.

"I'm the father?" he asked. "How is that possible?"

I arch a brow. "Sperm. Egg. Fertilization. Do you need a lesson in basic human biology?"

He shakes his head. "But we used a condom."

"Yeah, I know. Except for that false start."

He winces. "Oh. And that was enough?"

"Seems like it." I sigh. "It was a shock to me too." As

6

an athlete, I'm used to my cycle being irregular. It wasn't until two months after we'd shared our night together, when the morning sickness struck like a bitch, that I began to get an inkling of what might be going on.

"I bet it was."

I drop my hand from his arm, resisting the urge to stroke his tousled hair off his forehead. "Sorry for dumping it on you like that."

He exhales shakily. "You have nothing to be sorry for. I don't think there's a right way to give someone that news."

I nod because he's echoing my earlier thoughts. "You have a point."

We fall silent for a moment. I watch emotions play over his face, still struggling to believe I've run into him like this. I wanted to get in touch, but because of my stupid rule about not exchanging names, I had no way of contacting him. I went to the bar where we met a few times, hoping he'd show up, but he never did. Eventually I just figured I'd have to do this parenting thing alone.

I'm honestly not sure whether to be relieved or not by his sudden appearance. It will be nice to have someone to lean on, but he introduces a factor of uncertainty. Will he want to be involved? If so, will he try to change the way I'm doing things?

His gaze rakes over my midsection. "You're sure it's mine?"

"Completely." I'm not insulted he's asked. In his shoes, I would too. "You're the only man I've been with in the past nine months. Since I'm six months pregnant, that makes you the guilty party."

"Right. Okay." His frown deepens. "Why didn't you tell me sooner?"

I give him a look. "Was I supposed to run a Google search for Mr. Tattoos?"

"Oh yeah. The name thing." He holds out his hand. "Nice to meet you properly. I'm Mercy Caruso."

"Mercy," I muse. As I reach for him, something in my back spasms and I wince. The extra baby weight is starting to make itself known through the occasional ache or pain. "Caruso is Italian, right?"

"Yeah. My grandparents emigrated from Italy not long after they married."

"Well, it's nice to officially meet you, Mercy Caruso with the Italian grandparents. I'm Temperance Larson, but everyone calls me Tempe."

"It suits you." His frown eases slightly. "Let's go to my room so we can talk more."

"Sure. Lead the way."

He starts walking. I follow close behind, waddling a little. It's frustrating that the grace I worked so hard to attain after joining Crown MMA Gym is nowhere to be found. Pregnancy has wiped out a lot of my progress. I keep telling myself I can earn it back, but it won't be easy. It's especially difficult to accept because pregnancy wasn't part of my plan. Half the reason I broke up with my ex was that he wanted children and I wasn't ready. Someday, sure. But not until my career was more established. Then fate intervened and changed everything.

He unlocks the door and holds it open while I enter, then lets go of his suitcase and flops onto the bed. He pats the spot beside him. "Sit. I need a moment to gather my thoughts."

I laugh because I feel like I've been trying to gather my damn thoughts since I first saw those two little lines on the pregnancy test. I cross to the bed and perch on the edge. "I know how you feel."

Chapter Two

MERCY

This is actually happening.

Fuck. I've gotten a woman pregnant. I mean, I've always known it's a risk when I sleep with someone, but I wrap up every single time. Except for those first couple of thrusts with Tempe. A memory flashes through my mind. Me, slicking the head of my dick through the center of her wet pussy. Notching at the entrance and pushing in. Groaning because it felt so good. Then realizing I hadn't put the condom on yet and battling to pull out—both against my own urges and the tight grip she had on my ass. But I'd done it. I'd been inside her bare for less than five seconds. Apparently, I'd been leaking enough precum to do the job.

I turn to look at the curve of Tempe's belly. Her abdomen had been flat when we made love. Not only flat, but lightly muscled. Now, there's no denying the fact she's pregnant. And she's been dealing with it alone. For months, she's had to face up to what this pregnancy means —its disruption of her life—without the support of a partner. Even though there's no way I could have known, I feel like an ass for not being there for her. I should have said fuck her rules and insisted we swap contact details in case something like this happened. I dig my thumb into the muscles at the side of my jaw, which are starting to ache from clamping my teeth.

"I'm sorry you've had to go this alone," I tell her. "I'll be there every step of the way from now on."

Her eyes widen almost imperceptibly. "Thank you."

Is she surprised I'm willing to step up? She shouldn't be. It wouldn't be the first time. When my parents died in a car accident during my first year of college, I dropped out to raise my younger sister, Lucia. If I could do that at nineteen, then I can do the same for my own kid.

I maneuver myself into a seated position, resting against the wall at the head of the bed. "How is the pregnancy going? Have you had any problems? Have you been seeing the doctor?"

She draws back and her eyebrows knit together. "Everything is under control."

"Good. Thank you for taking care of our baby." My eyes slide to her belly once again and my head spins. I can hardly fathom that the tiny life growing inside her shares my DNA. "You don't need to worry about me flaking out on you. I'll do whatever I can. I'll be there for emotional and financial support." Although God only knows how, considering my dire financial situation. I'll make it work somehow because letting her and the baby down is not an option. "I want to be part of our child's life."

Her lips part and she blinks at me. Then she sucks in a breath. "I don't expect you to drop everything and take care of me. I just thought you deserved to know." She fidgets with the hem of her shirt. "I'm not even sure I want to keep the baby. I hadn't planned on having children until my career is off the ground. I've been thinking about putting her up for adoption."

"Her?" I ask, my mind catching on that because I can't even process the other half of what she said. "It's a girl?"

She shakes her head. "I meant that in a general sense. I haven't asked what the gender is. I want it to be a surprise. Although I might need to find out in order to get an adoption lined up." She hesitates. "Maybe you'd prefer to know anyway?"

"No, a surprise is fine." I don't want her to think I'm going to second-guess every decision she's made so far. I rub my temples. My brain is struggling to keep up. First, I have to deal with the fact I'm about to be a father, and then I find out that maybe I won't be after all if she decides to give the baby up for the sake of her career.

"What do you do?" I ask, realizing I never asked during our night together.

She grimaces. "I'm a professional fighter. Obviously, being pregnant has thrown my plans off. I haven't been able to fight, and my training is restricted to lower impact exercises."

There's a twinge of sympathy in my chest. Becoming successful as a female athlete must be challenging on the best of days, but having something like this thrown at her could be devastating. No wonder she's not sure if she wants to keep the baby. That said, I don't want her to make any decisions without me. Even if she's been handling things alone so far, the baby will be as much mine as hers, and I want a voice in what happens with them.

"I'm sorry," I say. "That must be frustrating."

She buries her face in her palms. "You have no idea."

I lay a hand on her shoulder, half-expecting her to shrug me off, but she doesn't. "I want to help."

Her shoulders stiffen and she drops her hands. "There's not much to do. I'm managing the best I can."

"Okay." I stop touching her. She's clearly tense, and having a stranger in her personal space might not be what she wants. "We'll need to discuss whether or not to put the baby up for adoption together. Not now, obviously, but I don't want you making that decision on your own. I'm their parent too and I have a right to be involved." This might not be what she wants to hear, but I need to say it.

She's quiet for a moment, then nods. "Fair enough."

Tension radiates from her body, and I wonder if she's afraid I'm going to try to force her to raise the child. I would never do that. If I decide I want to keep the baby and she doesn't, then I'll file for sole custody and raise them myself. I have no idea how, considering I'm broke as fuck and work all hours of the day, but I'm a resourceful guy. I can figure something out.

———

TEMPE

My mind tells me I should be grateful Mercy is willing to be involved, but my heart can't help feeling as if he's going to come in and take over. I've had enough of that in my previous relationship. I don't need it from a man I hardly know. I run a hand over the fine rows of braids on the top of my head and sigh. During our night together, I found Mercy's take-charge attitude sexy, but in real life, I don't want an alpha male trying to make decisions for me. No matter how well-intentioned he might be.

"Here's the thing," I say, meeting his incredible blue eyes. "I appreciate the show of support, and you're right; you have a right to help decide what happens next. But I've been working my ass off for my whole life to build this career and I won't have someone else telling me what to do with my body or my future."

"That's not—"

"Hold that thought." I don't let him complete the sentence. "We can talk it through and figure out the details, but like you said, this weekend isn't the time to do it. It's Hazel's wedding, and I'm not going to be one of those shitty bridesmaids who make it all about my personal drama. The baby won't go anywhere over the next few days, so how about we get together back in Las Vegas and make a plan?"

His chin sets mutinously. "I respect that it's our friends' wedding, but you can't just drop a bombshell on me and expect me not to talk about it at all."

"That's not what I'm doing," I protest, then sigh, realizing he might have a point. But doesn't he see this is hard for me too? "Yeah, okay. If there's anything you want to ask or say, you can. All I'm suggesting is that we don't rush ourselves. We have twelve weeks until the baby is due. Plenty of time to figure out the details."

"Okay." He nods. "We can put off the big conversation until after the wedding, but Isiah and Hazel deserve to know the truth too. I don't want them to be blindsided when the whole story comes out."

I wince. I hadn't considered that. My friends all know I got pregnant by a one-night stand, but the fact he's also a friend of theirs adds a layer of awkwardness. "You're right. We need to tell them. Do you want to do it together?"

"Yes." His voice is firm. "Why don't we go see them now? It's early enough that they can get over it before their wedding day."

My chest tightens. I can't believe how quickly this is happening after it's just been me and the corncob for the past six months. That's how big the baby is at this stage. The size of an ear of corn. I've taken to monitoring their progress according to a fruit and vegetable-based chart.

I weigh our options. Despite my apprehension, I see no reason to delay telling them. The sooner we break the news, the sooner they can recover from the shock and move on.

"Okay. Let's go." I stand and offer him a hand, but he shakes his head, casting a sideways glance at my stomach, and clambers to his feet. I scowl. I hate when people treat me like I'm fragile. I may be pregnant, but I could still kick his ass if I wanted.

We leave his room and we're halfway along the corridor when a man comes the other way. He's looking at his phone, but I recognize him instantly, and all the warmth flees my body, leaving me with a cold pit of dread in my gut.

Chad glances up and stops in his tracks, his dark eyes widening. "Tempe?"

I open my mouth but can't think of anything to say. I knew he was going to be here. He's in the bridal party because he and the groom are college friends—that's how we met—but I'd hoped our first interaction would be on my terms. Not standing in public with my pregnant belly on full display, accompanied by the man responsible for it. My shoulders hunch inward. I wish I could shrivel into a ball and disappear as Chad's gaze travels down my body and settles on my midsection. I watch as he realizes I'm pregnant by someone else after refusing to go down that track with him. Hurt flickers across his face, and even though things ended badly between us, I hate that I'm the cause of it.

"Chad, let me explain."

He falls back a step, his jaw working furiously as no sound comes out. Finally, he sputters, "You can't be serious. What happened to 'I'm not ready for a baby, Chad?' " His tone turns whiny as he mimics me. "Or was it just that *I* wasn't good enough to knock you up, but some other guy is?" His nostrils flare and he squares his shoulders. "You must have moved on pretty fucking quickly to be this far along. Or had you already started fucking someone else before we broke up?"

14

Chapter Three

MERCY

I step between Tempe and Chad. "Don't speak to her like that."

I'm not completely sure what's going on, but it's obvious they dated at some point and he's angry she's pregnant. Based on what she said about not having been with anyone in the past nine months, I assume they broke up at least a couple of months before we slept together. Either that or their sex life was dead before they ended things. I like that possibility because it would mean the problems would have been all on his side. Tempe was wild in bed with me.

"You." Chad's expression turns thunderous. Despite us having a mutual friend in Isiah, we've never liked each other. He thinks I'm a thug, and I think he's a pretentious dick, but we tolerate each other when we have to. "This is none of your business. Get the hell out of here. Tempe and I need to talk."

"Actually." I raise a hand to calm him but it seems to have the opposite effect. "It is my business, because she's my business." I meet her eyes, and she gives me a slight nod. I take a deep breath and say something I never thought I would. "The baby is mine."

He freezes. A dozen emotions flicker across his face, then he slowly turns to Tempe. "Say it isn't true."

She looks like a rabbit caught in the headlights of an oncoming truck, but she nods. "It is."

Chad spins around and kicks the wall. "Fuck!" He stands with his back to us for a few seconds, visibly getting a hold of himself before pivoting again. His expression has been schooled into a mask of nothingness. "I thought you were better than that."

"Hey," I snap. "Don't be a dick."

"Fuck off, Mercy."

Tempe frowns and glances between us. "You two have met before?"

"We're both friends with Isiah," I explain. "Although not so much with each other."

"Yeah, I'm getting that." She addresses Chad. "I'm sorry you're hurting; I never meant for that to happen. But this has nothing to do with you." She closes the distance to reach him and touches his arm. I fight the urge to put myself between them again. Whatever she says next is soft enough that I can't hear it, but Chad seems to deflate. He nods once and walks away. It's only when Tempe returns to my side that I notice she's shaking.

"You okay?" I ask.

She closes her eyes for a moment. When she opens them again, she's calmer. "I will be. I just wasn't expecting that. This whole afternoon is a clusterfuck." She grimaces apologetically. "Don't get me wrong, I'm glad you're here, but this is not how I thought my ex would find out I'm pregnant."

Yeah, as much of a shock as I've had, I can tell it's taken a toll on her too.

"Want a hug?" I ask. "I feel like we could both use one."

She sniffs and blinks suspiciously moist eyes. "Yes, please."

I gather her in my arms but don't hold her too tightly because I'm worried about squashing her stomach. I inhale deeply and catch a hint of a minty scent. My body clenches in response, my cock threatening to get hard. I recognize her smell from the night we spent together. I didn't realize it at the time, but it's probably some kind of liniment she uses during her training.

Calm the fuck down, I tell my overeager body. *We're doing this to support her, not get her naked.*

Honestly, as messed up as this whole situation is, I wouldn't mind getting her naked again. But I can't let that get in the way of doing the right thing. Standing by her side through the pregnancy is what's most important. My physical cravings don't even make the list.

——————

TEMPE

Do not cry on the nice man's shoulder.

Do not cry on the nice man's shoulder.

Oh, but it's such a wonderfully strong shoulder. I bet it could hold up the weight of all my problems. I can't just dump everything on him, though. Mercy has enough going on without me unloading all of my chaotic thoughts. I allow myself three more seconds of soaking up the comfort he's offering, and then I straighten and swipe at my eyes, grateful they haven't spilled over. I've been crying more easily lately.

"We should go and tell Hazel and Isiah," I say. "Chad agreed not to mention it tonight, but he's terrible at keeping his mouth shut, so we should hurry just in case."

"Is that what you said to him before?" he asks.

"Yeah." But I don't completely trust my ex. He's harboring a lot of anger toward me right now. I loop my arm through Mercy's. "Come on."

We find Hazel on the same sofa she'd been occupying earlier. She stands as we approach. Karen stays seated.

"Hazel, would you mind getting Isiah?" I ask, sending her a look that begs her not to ask questions.

"Of course." She stares at our looped arms curiously. "Just give me a couple minutes to track him down."

She heads off, and I usher Mercy onto the nearest sofa.

Karen leans forward, her gaze latched on to the place where our bodies touch as we sit. "I didn't realize you two knew each other." She's clearly fishing for information, but she'll have to wait until Hazel returns.

"We'll explain soon." Mercy glances at me as he says it, silently checking in. I tilt my head, letting him know I agree with his choice not to tell her before the others arrive. Unfortunately, Karen only seems more intrigued. We wait in charged silence until footsteps on the tiles indicate the bride and groom are here. Isiah claps Mercy on the shoulder as he passes, then settles onto the sofa opposite us, beside Karen. Hazel stands behind him.

"Great to see you," Isiah says. "Glad you could make it. It feels like ages since we got together."

"A few months at least," Mercy agrees.

"So, what's going on?" Isiah gestures between me and Mercy. "Hazel is dying of curiosity."

I bite my lip and rub my stomach protectively. Three sets of eyes follow the movement. I'm trying to figure out the best way to come clean when Mercy beats me to the punch.

"I'm the father of Tempe's baby."

Hazel's mouth falls open. She looks shell-shocked. "Oh my God."

"What the hell, man?" Isiah demands. "You got my fiancée's friend pregnant?"

"He didn't know who I was," I interject, not wanting to cause any problems in their relationship. "Like I told you, it was a one-night stand. I had no idea he'd be here, and he had no idea I'm pregnant."

"I'm still trying to come to terms with it," Mercy says. "But we wanted to let you know right away." He twines his fingers with mine and squeezes. Something inside me loosens. It feels good not to be in this alone anymore—even if I'm afraid of how all my plans might change.

"Thanks, I guess…" Isiah obviously doesn't know what to say. "Sorry, it's going to take a while to get my head around this. You two met in a bar?"

"Yeah." I'm the one to take the lead this time. "I told him I didn't want to exchange names or personal information."

Hazel shakes her head. "I can't imagine you doing something like that."

I look down at our joined hands, embarrassment heating my cheeks. "I wanted to forget Chad, so I went to the bar and chose the hottest guy there."

"I'll say," Karen agrees a little too enthusiastically. "With your combined genetics, you guys are going to have a gorgeous baby."

Hazel shoots her a look, and Karen quiets down. "Well, this week certainly isn't going to be boring." Her gaze journeys between us. "Are you going to tell Chad?"

"We already did," Mercy replies. "We saw him on our way over here."

I wince. "He was pretty upset."

Isiah sighs. "Poor guy. The last few months have been rough on him."

I don't point out they've been rough on me too. Isiah's primary concern is his friend.

"They haven't been a walk in the park for Tempe either," Hazel retorts, coming to my defense the way she always has.

Isiah holds his hands up in a peacemaking gesture. "I didn't mean anything by it."

"It's fine," I say before Hazel has the chance to respond. The last thing I want is to cause a fight between them two days before their wedding. "I understand. I feel bad for him too." Even if he's behaving poorly.

"Forget him." Hazel comes around to stand in front of me but speaks to the wider group. "We have dinner in a couple of hours. Why don't we all get a bit of space until then? I think we need it."

"That might be for the best," Isiah agrees.

Hazel offers me a hand. "I'll walk you to your room."

She meets Karen's eyes and shakes her head, indicating for her to stay put. I smile weakly as Hazel leads me away. Honestly, I wouldn't have minded Karen joining us, but Hazel needs to feel like she's in charge, so I don't say anything. The way Karen looks from me to Mercy and widens her eyes, then winks, I doubt her feelings are hurt. She's going to be asking for details as soon as she can get me alone.

"See you later," I say to the others. When we get to my room, I lie gingerly on the bed while Hazel sits cross-legged on the chair in the corner. We talk until it's nearly time for dinner. I tell her more about what happened between me and Mercy earlier in the evening, and when she leaves to prepare for the meal, I grab my phone and message my friend Ashlin, who's become a lifeline for me. She's recently given birth to a son, and she's the only friend I have who can offer advice on pregnancy.

Tempe: *I found the father.*

Ashlin: *Oh my God. Where?*

Tempe: *At my friend's wedding. He's a groomsman.*

Ashlin: *What a weird coincidence. How did he react?*

Tempe: *He seems to be handling it well. I hope he doesn't try to take charge too much though.*

Ashlin: *That's good. Here's a tip. When it comes to dealing with alpha males, you just need to get clear on what you want, tell them, and then not budge on it. Take it from someone who knows.*

Tempe: *Thanks. I'm off to dinner with him, the bride and groom, and my ex. Wish me luck!*

Ashlin: *You don't need luck. You need a miracle. I have my fingers crossed for you!*

Chapter Four

MERCY

After a sleepless night, I eat breakfast and seek out Tempe. She's walking among the vines. The air hasn't warmed yet, and the temperature is mild as I wind through the rows of grapes toward her.

"Good morning."

She turns and smiles. The side view of her stomach takes my breath away, and I feel itchy and restless in my own skin. That's *my* baby in there. Mine. And I know how caveman it makes me that I have a temporary moment of satisfaction before the nerves kick into gear, but I can't help it.

"Morning," she says, then winces.

"What is it?" I ask, because something is wrong. "Does your back hurt?"

"Just enough to be annoying." She pulls a face. "The baby is growing to the point where the extra weight seems to put pressure on everything. I've been hoping she stops growing soon, but based on what happened with my friend, Ashlin, I think I'm out of luck. She ballooned in her third trimester."

"Is that what you're in?" I mentally curse myself for not knowing more about pregnancy. My knowledge of what happens between conception and birth is pretty much nonexistent, other than morning sickness and the baby bump. I make a note to rectify that situation later.

"Yeah, just."

"Is there anything I can do to make you more comfortable? I can get you a Tylenol." I'd offer a back rub but I don't want to cross any boundaries between us.

"Thanks, but no." She rolls her shoulders and grimaces. "I'm trying to keep things as natural as possible for the little one, which means no medication unless I absolutely need it."

I hate how useless that makes me feel. She's experiencing discomfort as a result of something I played an equal role in, yet there's nothing I can do about it. I wish I could share the load. That's what I like to do—make things easier for others. But so far, all I've done for Tempe is make things harder.

My eyes track back to her belly, and something pinches in my chest. I've always wanted kids. Not under these circumstances perhaps, but I'm in my thirties so it's not as though I'm too young. Now is as good a time as any. A rush of emotion blasts through me. Suddenly, I want the baby she's carrying with an intensity that stuns me. I'd already decided as I lay in bed last night that nobody else will be raising my child, but I didn't feel the same visceral yearning I do now. I want to see tiny fingers and toes, a cute nose, and the brown eyes I assume our baby will have.

I take a step toward her. "I know we agreed to wait until next week to discuss anything major, but I have so much going on in my head. I need to get some of it out into the open."

She nods. "All right. That's okay. I cycled through every

freaking emotion you can think of when I found out I was pregnant. What's bothering you?"

"I want to keep our baby." The words spill from my mouth with no finesse, and she looks taken aback. "I'd never try to force you to be involved after the birth," I hasten to add, in case she thinks that's what I'm doing. "If you decide you're not ready to be a mother, then let me take her. Don't put her up for adoption."

She holds my gaze for a moment as though trying to determine whether I'm sincere. "Okay. But I want you to confirm next week that you still feel the same after you've had more time to think about it."

"I can do that." I understand why she doesn't want me to make a rushed decision. If I change my mind, it will impact her.

"I'll try to decide what I want within the next month so you can start making plans," she says.

"Thank you." Not that it matters to a certain extent. Yeah, it'll be good to know, but however things shake out, I'm going to have to conjure money out of thin air. I don't tell her that, though, because she has enough on her mind without me confessing to my money troubles. I'll clear the debt I've accumulated as a result of Danny's illness and death. Somehow. "Which way are you leaning at the moment?"

She shrugs, looking a little lost. "Honestly, I'm not sure. My career has always been the most important thing in my life, but I've had months with this little guy growing inside me and the idea of giving him up hurts like hell. Maybe it's a hormonal thing, but they feel like a part of me."

I nod. "I can't pretend I know what it's like to be pregnant, but I'm already attached to her, and I only found out she exists yesterday, so I get where you're coming from." I hesitate and then ask one of the questions I've been

24

mulling over. "If you could go back in time and undo our night together, would you?"

She cocks her head, and I can see a dozen thoughts flash through her dark eyes. She reaches up and idly pats a braid back into place before answering. "It would definitely uncomplicate my future. But we had the best sex of my life. It was exactly what I needed at the time, and I can't regret meeting you." Her full lips curve. "I actually kinda like you, baby daddy."

"I kinda like you too." Her words are great for my ego. That night topped all others for me, but considering she didn't stick around, I wasn't sure she'd felt the same. "Would you ever have thought about having more than a one-night stand with me? Because I wanted to see more of you, but you vanished."

Her teeth sink into her lower lip, and she rolls it while she thinks. "If I hadn't been fresh out of a bad relationship, then you would have been everything I was looking for." She exhales heavily. "But with the way things were, I wasn't in a good headspace for anything more than a one-off." She moves closer, and I catch a waft of her minty scent. "That had nothing to do with you and everything to do with me. Got it?"

"Got it." Except I can't help staring at her lips. They're so plush, and I remember how soft they were beneath my mouth and around my dick. Even as I try to convince myself to leave her alone, I can't help admiring her strength. She's been completely honest with me from the moment we saw each other yesterday, even when it can't have been easy for her. She's fucking incredible.

I sigh. "I really want to kiss you. Is that messed up?"

She laughs. "I want to kiss you too, but it's a terrible idea. Everything is so much more complicated than last time."

"So, the kissing is a no?"

Her eyes twinkle. "I didn't say that."

I cup her face between my palms. She lets out a little gasp, and my insides tighten with anticipation. "Can I kiss you, Miss Mystery?"

"Yes, Mr. Tattoos. Apparently, when it comes to you, I like complicated."

I'm smiling when my mouth touches hers. We kiss softly at first, but then she whimpers and presses closer. My arms twine around her, and I lick the seam of her lips, delving into her mouth. Our tongues brush and it ignites something inside of me. Her fingers dig into my arms as she grips me, and in that moment, nothing could drag me away. But then she draws back. I follow, my mind fuzzy and kiss-drunk.

"Wait," she whispers. "I hear something."

I pause and listen. She's right. There are voices approaching—perhaps from around the side of the lodge. We're partially out of view among the vines, but our heads are on full display and we probably shouldn't get caught making out by anyone in the bridal party. I cast her one last, longing glance, then release her. Damn it.

———

TEMPE

I'm in so much trouble. If not for the people about to come around the corner, I'd happily kiss Mercy until we ran out of oxygen. I'm secretly pleased our chemistry is still present after all this time, but it doesn't make things easier. I'm having a hard enough time trying to balance my life without adding a new relationship to the mix. Because that's what anything between us would have to be. I won't risk having a fling with my baby's father. There's too much that could go wrong. Perhaps it's just as well we were interrupted before I could check whether he's on the same page, though. He might think the fact I'm already pregnant gives us a good excuse for no-strings sex. I doubt it, though. He doesn't seem like that kind of guy.

I take a few steps away from him and pat my hair to make sure it's all in place. When Chad's face appears around the corner, closely followed by Isiah, Hazel, and Karen, I'm glad for the distance I put between us. Chad crinkles his nose as though he's smelled something bad. Isiah looks decidedly uncomfortable to have found us together. But when I scan the women's faces, I see Hazel's is speculative and Karen's is downright gleeful. Karen glances at the others as if to make sure they're not paying attention to her, then gives me a subtle thumbs-up. I can't help but grin. She's ridiculous, but she's a fun person to be around. I start heading toward them and Mercy follows.

"Good morning." I smile. "Where have you all come from?"

"Breakfast," Hazel replies. "Did you eat?"

I laugh. "Yeah, I was up at dawn because the little one needed food."

"What about you, Mercy?" Hazel asks.

"I ate." He shifts his weight, stirring the air beside me, and my arms prickle with awareness. "But I wanted to catch Tempe before we got started on the day's events, so I didn't hang around for long."

Chad's expression darkens. Before I've noticed his intention, he's closed the space between us and grabbed my hand. "Can I talk to you in private?"

Mercy moves closer to me. "Not a good idea."

"It's okay." I can't avoid a difficult conversation with Chad forever. We need to clear the air. "You guys go on. We'll catch up with you soon. It's the wine tasting in ten minutes, right?"

Hazel nods. "I've arranged for them to have nonalcoholic sparkling grape juice available too."

27

"Thank you. You're amazing."

"You're welcome."

The group moves away but Mercy doesn't budge. Chad glares at him, but Mercy raises his chin and grabs my hand. "I'm not going anywhere." He eyeballs Chad. "Stress isn't good for the baby, so be careful what you say."

Chad snorts. "Look at you. Acting as if you know anything. Didn't you only find out yesterday?"

"Children," I snap. "Cut it out." They're like a pair of dogs sniffing each other, trying to figure out who's the alpha.

"Sorry, Tempe." Chad seems chastened. "I just don't understand anything that's happening here."

"You don't have to," Mercy informs him, but I soften. Chad isn't a bad guy. He's just having a hard time with this, as many people would.

"The details of what happened between Mercy and I are private," I remind Chad. "But it's safe to say we didn't expect this." I resist the urge to take his hand to try to make him feel better. That isn't my role. "I'm sorry you're upset by the way things have played out, but I'd appreciate it if you could be respectful, because frankly, what I do, and whom I'm with isn't your business anymore."

He stares for a moment, stunned by my bluntness. I've always tiptoed around him. But while I want to be polite, I need to make the boundaries clear, or this entire weekend is going to be awkward for everyone. Mercy squeezes my hand in a silent display of support.

"Yeah, okay." Chad falls back a step. "I guess I've been thinking of myself as the wounded party, but you're right —it has nothing to do with me." One side of his mouth curls into a smile that's a little sad. "I just have a hard time accepting that."

To my surprise, Mercy speaks. "I didn't know who she was to you when we met. No hard feelings?"

Chad's chest rises as he inhales. I'm not sure how he's going to respond, but then he releases the breath and nods. "Take care of her, or we'll have a problem."

"I will."

"Good. I'll be watching." Chad meets my eyes. "I'm sorry for how I spoke to you yesterday."

Holding on to resentment won't do me any good. "Forgiven."

The other side of his mouth curls up. "Thanks. I think I'll head over to the tasting room. See you soon." With that, he walks off, leaving us alone.

I turn to Mercy, amazed by how composed he is. There's a niggle of worry in my gut that he's suppressing his emotions and burying any concerns about what comes next.

"Is there anything else you want to talk about before we join them?" I ask.

"No." He's impossible to read, but I still try. "Why don't we catch up with the others?"

Together, we stroll in the direction the others went earlier, but inside, the niggle of worry has grown into a knot. How am I supposed to know what's going on in his head if he doesn't tell me?

Chapter Five

Mercy

The rest of the wedding passes in a blur. I go to all the right places, say and do all the right things, but I'm mentally checked out. I'm too busy mulling over how to afford a baby and what I can do to make room for one in my life. I own a small tattoo parlor and work from early morning until late at night to keep it going. The business has a good reputation and does well, but I'm on the back foot after fronting Danny's medical bills and losing him as an artist.

The only person capable of distracting me from my frantic mental maneuvering is Tempe. Every time I see her, I want to touch her and taste her. But the craving isn't only physical. I want to hold her and ask her about her dreams so I can figure out how to make them a reality. Unfortunately, we aren't alone together often. We sneak a few kisses but don't get the chance to talk about what we're doing with each other or whether to take it further. By the time the newly married couple leave for their honeymoon, Tempe and I have made plans to see each other on Monday in Las Vegas. I return home, exhausted and ready to sleep in my own bed. If I can sleep at all. I've barely caught a wink since we first ran into each other.

When I pull up outside my small rental house in one of the quieter parts of the city, my sister's car is parked on the street. I smile. Even when I'm tired as hell, I love seeing Lucia. Sometimes she feels more like my daughter than my sister. Especially considering I raised her through her teenage years. I wheel my suitcase to the door and try the handle. It's unlocked. Opening it, I let myself in. I leave the suitcase in my bedroom and follow the hall through the house to the living room, where Lucia is lying on the sofa, reading a paperback. She looks up as I enter and then grins.

"How did the wedding go?" She scans my face. "You look shattered."

"I feel shattered," I reply. "It was lovely. But something happened."

She swings her feet to the floor. "What is it? Are you okay?"

I flop onto the other end of the sofa. "Yeah." Honestly, "okay" probably isn't the right word, but there's no need to worry her. Everything will be under control soon, one way or another. "Do you remember me mentioning the woman I met at a bar about six months ago?"

Lucia frowns. "The one you were moping about for weeks?"

I wince. Moping isn't very manly. "I was disappointed I didn't get the chance to see her again."

"Uh-huh." She gives me a look that sisters worldwide have been giving their brothers for millennia. "Okay. What about her?"

"She was at the wedding. Apparently she's one of Hazel's childhood friends."

"That's great! I hope you did something about it."

I scrunch my nose. "It's a bit more complicated than that."

"How so?"

"She's pregnant."

"Oh." She sighs. "That's a shame. The way you talked about her, I thought she might be the one for you."

I press my lips together so I don't laugh at her mention of "the one." Lucia is such a romantic. She believes in soul mates and happily ever after. I'm glad losing our parents young didn't rob her of that. "Luce, the baby is mine. She got pregnant during our night together."

Lucia's eyes bulge with shock. "But... what?" She points at me accusingly. "Didn't you use protection?"

"Of course." As if I'd ever go without. "But it's not foolproof. And now I'm going to be a father."

"Oh my God." She rubs her temples. "I can't believe what I'm hearing." She stares at me. "Are we happy about this? Angry? Confused? Sad?"

I rest my head against the cushion. "I don't even know. Not angry. It isn't her fault. Everything is just so mixed up, and I'm not sure what to make of it."

She opens her mouth, then hesitates.

"What?" I ask.

She squirms in her seat. "Are you sure it's your baby?" She looks like she'd rather do anything other than ask, but she puts it out there anyway. "I know what you're like. You leap at the chance to play white knight."

I don't dismiss the question even though I want to. It's a legitimate concern, and the possibility had crossed my mind for a few seconds before I saw how genuine Tempe was. "I'm sure. She wouldn't do that. But I'll ask for a paternity test anyway because if she decides she doesn't want the baby, then I'll file for full custody. Having proof of paternity will help my case."

"Good. That's sensible." She sighs. "So, wow. I wasn't expecting that news when you arrived back tonight."

"I found out four days ago, and I'm still not sure I've got my head around it," I admit. "It's crazy."

"You can say that again." She draws her knees to her chest, studying me with pale blue eyes that are so like my own. "You said she might not want the baby. What kind of person wouldn't want their own child?"

I can see her disdain loud and clear. She already thinks Tempe is a bad mother. But then, Lucia's big dream in life is to have a home, a husband, and a tribe of children. She's always wanted that and can't imagine the thought of someone else throwing it all away. But she needs to understand not everyone shares her values or perspective.

"She's a professional athlete," I say. "As far as I can tell, she's worked her ass off to make something of herself in a male-dominated sport, and she doesn't want to lose everything. Being pregnant has set her back months from where she'd otherwise be."

"Huh." Her frown eases. "I didn't expect that either. Has she said whether she's against having children in general?"

"We didn't discuss it, but as far as I can tell, she's not. The timing is just bad for her."

Lucia presses her lips together. "That must be difficult. Do you think she'll decide to keep the baby?"

I shrug. "I have no idea."

Even though I tell myself I can handle whatever decision she makes, I want her to decide to be part of this baby's life. Not just because it would make things easier for me, but because I want to see more of her. This weekend didn't satisfy my curiosity about Tempe. Or my hunger for her. I want the opportunity to explore whatever is happening between us and see where it goes. If I raise our baby without her, then we'll most likely have to cut ties, and I'll always wonder what might have been.

"I want to meet her," Lucia says. "If this woman is going to be hanging around for the foreseeable future, then I'd like to get to know her." She pauses, then smiles mischievously. "I know it's unconventional, but perhaps this is the universe's way of bringing her back to you. You've always wanted a family."

An ache settles in my gut. I do want a family, more than she knows, but I'm afraid to hope because Tempe Larson has the power to hurt me, and my life is messy enough without trying to recover from a broken heart.

"Maybe," I reply noncommittally. "Or maybe not. I guess we'll see what happens next."

———

Tempe

I hold goddess pose, watching my teammates train on the main floor of the gym while I'm in the corner, doing goddamn yoga—and not just any yoga, but pregnant-woman yoga. The easiest and gentlest poses. Nothing that could possibly put strain on my body. Harley and Enya are sparring, and my insides knot with frustration. I wish I could be in their position. But no, I'm relegated to the corner because I don't want to risk anything happening to my baby. I love the corncob, even if they drive me freaking nuts sometimes.

As I scan the other pairs, spots dance in front of my eyes. I blink a few times and shake my head, but they don't go away. Weird. Maybe it's something to do with the position. I move out of goddess pose and into dancing warrior. But the spots don't leave. I take several breaths and decide to ignore them. All kinds of strange things have been happening to my body lately. It's probably nothing to worry about. I hold the pose for a while longer, then carefully lower myself to my knees to do some hip circles. As I do, a sharp pain wrenches my right side. I gasp at the sudden onset, barely able to breathe. My arm gives out beneath me, but I manage to stop myself from hitting the floor.

"*Fuck,*" I hiss, clutching my side. What's happening to me?

"Tempe, are you okay?" a guy asks from somewhere nearby. I can't tell who it is because all I'm able to focus on is the pain. It's beginning to fade, but there's a pulsing sensation that makes me worry it's going to come back worse.

"Something is wrong," I gasp. "Need to call Ashlin."

"I'll get your phone." The pain has dulled enough that I recognize my close friend Enya's voice when she speaks.

"Let me help you up." A muscular arm slides around my back and supports me as I struggle to my feet. I glance at the man's face. Through the haze of unshed tears, Tony's handsome features come into view. He assists me to a chair. I glance around, noticing we have an audience. Seth, my coach, is tapping a number into his phone. Most of the others look worried enough that my own anxiety grows.

"Here." Enya appears in front of me with my cell phone. "It's Ashlin."

Hearing this, Seth pockets his phone. He must have been calling Ashlin too. She's his wife. I wince as another bolt of pain shoots through me, then take the phone from Enya and speak into it.

"My side is killing me," I grit out. "I'm worried something is wrong with the baby."

"You need to see your doctor," Ashlin says. "You have health insurance, right?"

"Yeah." As a professional fighter, it's a pretty important

thing to have. "Are you sure it's that bad? I don't want to waste their time."

"Tempe." She sounds exasperated. "You're one of the toughest women I know. If you're in this much pain, you need professional help. Please be smart about this."

"Okay," I murmur. "I'll call her right now. Thanks."

"Take care of yourself," Ashlin replies.

I end the call and drop the phone onto my lap. Just speaking to her exhausted me.

"Tempe." Enya squats in front of me. "What do you need?"

I pass her my phone. "Can you please call Dr. Lang?"

"Of course." She steps away and a few moments later, I hear her speaking to someone. "Here." She presses the phone back into my palm. "It's her."

"Hi, Doc." I squeeze my eyes shut and breathe through a particularly painful throb. "I need to see you. Do you have any appointments available? It's urgent."

"Is everything okay?" She sounds concerned.

"No. I'm not sure what's wrong. There's a pain in my side, and my vision is playing up."

She's quiet for a moment. "Come in immediately. I'll have my assistant reschedule my next appointment so we can fit you in."

"Thank you." I'm beyond grateful. "See you soon."

"The sooner the better. Don't drive yourself. It might not be safe."

"I won't. Bye." I hang up and turn to Enya. "Can you take me to the hospital?"

"I'll drive," Tony offers, surprising me. "Enya can ride in the back with you."

I blink back tears. "Thank you both." I'm so lucky to have their support.

I hear murmurs of sympathy as I make my way

outside. Tony's arm comes around my back, guiding me to his sports car. He helps me into the front seat.

"My bag?" I ask.

"Enya has it." His tone is gentle. More so than I've ever heard it, and that scares me.

"Thanks." I'm vaguely aware of him getting into the driver seat and Enya climbing in beside me as I scroll through my phone, looking for Mercy's number. We exchanged details prior to separating yesterday. I select it and hit Call. It rings for so long, I'm afraid he won't answer, but thankfully he does.

"Hey, Miss Mystery," he says playfully.

I close my eyes, hating that he sounds so lighthearted when I'm about to pop his bubble. "Hi, Mercy. I'm having some stomach pain. My friends are taking me to the hospital. I thought you'd like to know."

"Shit. Are you okay?" I hear something clatter, and he curses.

"Not great, but I could be worse." I sense Enya giving me a skeptical look, and I ignore her. "I'm not sure if I'll be able to meet with you tonight."

"Don't worry about that." Muffled noises give me the impression he's moving. "I'll see you at the hospital."

"You don't have to come."

"I'll be there." His tone brooks no argument. "Which one?"

"Sunshine," I say, crooking a brow at Tony to make sure he knows where to go. He nods. "See you soon."

"You're going to be okay."

I almost smile because he says the words with authority, but we both know neither of us have any idea what's going on. "Bye, Mercy."

"Bye."

I end the call and pocket the phone.

"That was the guy from this weekend?" Enya asks, apparently unable to help herself. "The baby's father?"

"Yeah." I curl up as a fresh wave of pain rockets through me. "He'll meet us there."

"Good." She slips her hand into mine. "I know you can take care of yourself, but I'm glad someone else is finally around to help you."

"Me too," I whisper. Whatever roller coaster I'm embarking on, Mercy is strapped in alongside me. Perhaps he doesn't have to deal with the same physical aspects as me, but that's almost worse because he's powerless to do anything other than watch. I'd struggle in his shoes.

When Tony pulls up outside the hospital, Enya helps me out of the car. Tony leaves to find a parking spot, and we slowly make our way inside, where I direct Enya to Dr. Lang's wing. We advise the receptionist of our appointment, and she calls the doctor to let her know we've arrived. We hover there for a few moments, and then two men burst into the waiting area almost simultaneously. Tony and Mercy. When Mercy sees me, he rushes over and scans my body as though looking for any visible sign of harm, then he gently draws me into his arms. I rest my head on his chest and breathe in his faint antiseptic scent. He must have come directly from the tattoo parlor.

"I'm sorry if I interrupted an appointment," I say.

"You didn't." He strokes a hand down my back. "This is more important anyway."

"Wait, you're the one who got her pregnant?" It's Tony who's asked the question. "I didn't think you were the kind of guy to leave her high and dry for six months."

Mercy stiffens. "I only just found out."

"You guys know each other?" I ask.

"We've met a couple of times." Tony sounds like he's not sure how to take this news.

"Oh, right." It seems everyone knew who Mercy was

38

except for me. "Tony, Enya, thanks for bringing me, but you can probably go now." I glance at Mercy. "Can you take me home after?"

"Absolutely." He brushes his lips across my forehead, then turns to the others. "I appreciate you looking after her. I can take it from here if you need to get back to training."

Tony nods but Enya hesitates. "Are you going to be okay?" she asks.

"I think so." The pain is easing again, and the last thing she needs is for me to interrupt her training schedule. After winning her fight against a British champion several months ago, she's been in high demand and has a title fight on the horizon. "I'll let you know how it goes."

"Okay." She reluctantly steps away. "I'll check in as soon as I can."

"Thanks, girl."

A throat clears behind us. "Tempe, will you please come with me?"

Mercy steers me toward Dr. Lang, who has emerged from the corridor, her blonde hair disheveled and her scrubs crinkled. There are shadows under her eyes. I'm vaguely aware of Tony and Enya departing as we follow Dr. Lang into a room with a single bed.

"Please, sit."

I perch on the edge of the bed, trying to focus on the doctor's face, but spots dance in front of my eyes again, making it difficult. "Thank you for seeing me. This is Mercy. He's the dad."

"Nice to meet you." She gives me her attention. "Can you please walk me through what happened and how you're feeling?"

I repeat what I told her earlier.

"All right." She dons a pair of latex gloves. "Do you mind if I touch you? I need to palpate your abdomen."

I nod, regretting it when the world seems to swim in front of my eyes. "Go for it."

Dr. Lang touches her fingertips to my stomach gently but firmly. They travel over the bump and around my side. I wince when she touches a particularly tender area.

"Hmm." She straightens. "I'm going to measure your blood pressure."

She fits the blood pressure cuff around my arm and pumps it up. I can't tell from her face whether the reading is good or bad. She deflates the cuff and sets it aside. "Your blood pressure is high. Much higher than I'd expect for someone your age and physical fitness." She pauses for a moment, and I have a sinking feeling whatever she's about to say won't be good. "We'll need to take a urine sample to confirm, but I think it's likely you have a condition called preeclampsia. Have you heard of it?"

My chest tightens. I don't know exactly what preeclampsia is, but I've definitely heard of it, and I know it's not good. "I don't know much."

Mercy edges closer and takes my hand, offering silent support. "Tell us."

The doctor nods. "It usually happens in the third trimester, and it's characterized by high blood pressure, visual disturbance, and protein in the urine. The abdominal pain you experienced is another potential symptom."

Mercy's fingers curl around mine and squeeze. "What does it mean for her and the baby?"

Dr. Lang faces him. "It increases the risk of complications arising from the pregnancy until she goes through labor. It's not uncommon to induce labor after a diagnosis of preeclampsia when it occurs later in the pregnancy, but we want to avoid that at this stage if possible."

"Increased risk?" My heart is pounding, which can't be good for my already high blood pressure. "Does that mean I'm going to lose the baby?"

Dr. Lang's expression softens. "It's a possibility, but if we manage the rest of your pregnancy carefully, we can minimize the chance of that happening."

My skin prickles and sweat breaks out on my upper lip. "What do I have to do to keep my baby safe?"

"First off, we'll get that urine sample. Then, if it confirms my diagnosis, you'll need to rest for the remainder of the pregnancy." She sighs. "I'm sorry to say it, but that means no more training, and ideally, you should have someone around to monitor you in case you need to be brought into the hospital again."

No more training?

My heart falls. I've already had a hard enough time keeping up. But when I think of anything happening to the tiny life growing inside me, it breaks my heart. I already love my little one, so if I have to give up MMA for a few months, then I will. But I don't have to like it.

"Okay. I can do that."

Dr. Lang slants a sideways look at Mercy. "No vigorous sex either." He nods but doesn't mention the fact we're not a real couple. "Tempe, is there anyone living with you currently?" Again, her eyes travel to Mercy.

"No."

She presses her lips together. "Is there someone who can stay with you temporarily?"

"My sister probably can," I say before remembering Justine flew out of state for a conference over the weekend. She won't be back until next Sunday. "Wait, no. She can't."

"You can stay with me," Mercy says simply.

I stare at him. We barely know each other, and he's offering to act as my nursemaid? "Won't that be weird considering we're practically strangers?"

He twines his fingers between mine. "We might not be in a relationship, but we're having a baby, and I care about

41

you. I contributed equally to this situation, and I want to help. My sister, Lucia, works from home, and she could stay with you during the day while I have to be at the parlor. Unless you'd rather stay at your place, and we can join you there?"

I pull a face. "My apartment is pretty small. It was only supposed to be temporary, until I got back on my feet after the breakup with Chad. I've got a casual lease on it, and I hardly have any furniture since Chad kept everything. It would make more sense to go to yours, if there's room for me."

"There is. You can even bring your belongings, if you like. That way you don't have to keep paying the lease on your apartment while we work out a long-term arrangement."

I purse my lips and consider his offer. With Justine out of state and my parents back in Maryland, I don't have a heap of other options. I could stay with Enya, but she'd be away during the day. My only alternative would be to move in with Seth and Ashlin. But Ashlin has enough on her plate without worrying about me.

"Okay." My stomach churns uncomfortably at the thought of what comes next, and the ache in my side beats a pulsing rhythm. "I'll stay with you, but if it isn't working out for any reason, I'll find somewhere else to go. Does that work?"

He nods, a grim look of determination in his eyes. "Yes."

Chapter Six

Mercy

I've only known this baby exists for a few days, yet my emotions are in an uproar at the thought of losing them. I'm also shocked by how protective I feel of Tempe. When she called earlier, it wasn't just the possibility of something happening to the baby that had me terrified—I wanted *her* to be safe too. Perhaps it's because of the electric connection between us, but it feels right to take her in and care for her. It's not as though doing that is new for me—as Lucia likes to point out, I have a habit of helping strays. But this goes beyond that. I feel a fierce, burning need to ensure Tempe is happy and safe, and our baby gets the best start to life they possibly can.

"Okay, since we've got that sorted," Dr. Lang says, breaking the intense moment between us, "Tempe, can I get you to pee into this container?" She passes her a small plastic cup. Tempe cringes a little. "Do you need a hand getting to the bathroom? It's just over there." She waves a hand toward a side door.

"No, I'll be fine." Tempe strides away and I wait in awkward silence with the doctor until Tempe returns and places the container on the counter beside the bed. I don't look at it because I don't want to make her feel more embarrassed than she already is. She leans against the bed and I sit forward, so I can support her if needed.

"Perfect." Dr. Lang smiles. "I'll call to confirm the results, and in the meantime, someone will get in touch to work out a more frequent appointment schedule. We want to do everything we can to ensure you're healthy."

"Thank you," Tempe and I say at the same time.

"I'm also going to prescribe medication to lower your blood pressure," the doctor continues. She goes to her desk and messes around on the computer for a couple minutes, then prints a prescription and signs it. "Fill this at the hospital pharmacy before you leave."

Tempe's lips twitch with displeasure, and I recall her saying she wanted the pregnancy to be as natural as possible. She doesn't argue, though. She knows protecting the baby is the most important thing.

"Do you have any questions?" Dr. Lang asks.

Tempe gets straight to the point. "What are the chances of something going wrong?"

The doctor purses her lips. "Honestly, it's impossible to know for certain. It depends on a range of factors. All we can do is minimize the possibility."

"Are we talking fifty-fifty odds or something else?" I ask, wanting to know how precarious our situation is.

Dr. Lang's expression says she doesn't want to guess. "If we manage Tempe's condition and monitor her carefully, then most likely better than that, but there's no way to tell for sure."

I nod. "Okay, got it."

"Thanks, Doc." Tempe stands and I wrap an arm around her shoulders. "I appreciate you fitting me in."

"No problem at all." Dr. Lang walks us to the door. "Remember what I said: take it easy."

"I'll make sure she does," I reply, earning a scowl.

"Good. See you both next time."

We respond in kind, and Tempe and I head toward the hospital pharmacy.

"You know your way around," she says as we navigate the corridors.

"Yeah." Although I'd rather not think about why. "I've spent a bit of time here recently."

She takes me at face value and doesn't push for details, which I'm both grateful for and disappointed by. Talking about Danny is hard, but for some reason, I sense it would be a relief to share those memories with her. We arrive at the pharmacy and give the prescription to one of the staff members, who tells us it will be ready in ten minutes. We sit in the small waiting area.

"I'm going to call Lucia," I tell her. "I'll be back in a moment."

"Okay."

I walk far enough away that she shouldn't be able to overhear my conversation. I don't plan on saying anything she won't like, but I can't know for sure how Lucia will respond to the news, and I'd rather be safe than sorry. I grab my phone and select her number. It rings a few times before connecting.

"Hi," Lucia says.

"Hey, Luce. I have a massive favor to ask."

"What is it?" I can hear her wary curiosity through the line.

"I'm at the hospital. Tempe is having some complications with the pregnancy."

"Oh no! Is she okay?"

"At the moment. But she needs someone around to make sure she's safe for the rest of the pregnancy. She lives alone so I offered for her to stay with me."

"Mercy, you work during the day," she reminds me.

I grimace. "I was hoping you'd come over. You can work from my place just as well as yours, right?"

"Wait." She sounds surprised. "You want me to babysit your baby mama?"

"Is that a problem?"

"Pfft. Not at all. In fact, it's pretty much perfect. I can get to know her better and make sure she's a good match for you."

"We're not together," I caution.

"But you like her," she returns. "And she obviously liked you well enough to let you take her to bed at least once. Now she'll be living at your place while you care for her, and who knows what might happen?" She makes a swoony sound as though it's all just *so romantic*. "I'm telling you, this could be your happily ever after."

I shake my head. "You're crazy. But if it means you'll help, then I don't care. Just don't stress her out."

"I won't." Her voice rises excitedly. "We'll be best of friends before you know it."

The idea frightens me. "Can we pick you up soon? We'll need help collecting her car from the gym."

"She was training?"

"Yeah, but she won't be able to train again until after the birth."

"Ouch. That must be tough for her." She hums in thought. "I'll pack a bag and be ready whenever you're here."

"Great." I pause. "Thanks so much, Luce."

"Don't mention it. See you soon." She hangs up.

I rejoin Tempe, who's clutching a small paper bag.

"Everything okay?" she asks.

"Yeah. Just making sure my sister is on board with our plan."

"Thank you." She holds my gaze so I can see the sincerity in her eyes. "For everything."

"It's no problem at all."

We walk back to my car, then drive to Lucia's place. She's waiting on the steps with a suitcase and hurries over as soon as we stop.

"Hi!" She's talking before the door is fully open and shoves her suitcase onto the backseat. "You must be Tempe. I'm Lucia. It's so nice to meet you." She reaches over to awkwardly half-hug Tempe, who's in the passenger seat. "I'm sorry about your complications. I hope it's nothing serious."

"We won't know for sure until after they get the test results back," Tempe replies. "Thanks for dropping everything to help. I'm sorry to mess up your afternoon."

Lucia waves a hand dismissively. "All I was doing was writing a review of a new French restaurant. I can finish it from anywhere. It's far more interesting to meet you." She glances at Tempe's belly. "Is congratulations the right thing to say?"

To my surprise, Tempe smiles. "I suppose it is. At first, it didn't feel that way, but I've grown to love this little one."

"That's great." Lucia settles into her seat and I pull away from the curb.

My sister stays blessedly quiet until I drop her off at the gym, where Tempe hands over the keys to her car and gives a description of the make and model. The plan is for Lucia to drive it back to my place. Once we've left, Tempe gives me her address. I follow her directions and park outside. It's a nondescript apartment building. When we enter, I can tell why she doesn't mind moving to my house. It's clear she hasn't made herself at home here. It takes only a few minutes for her to pack everything she'll need into a duffel bag. I try to convince her to sit on the sofa while I do the work, but she won't have it. Eventually, I give in and keep a close watch on her. When we've got everything she needs, we drive the last leg of our journey to my place. She studies it through the window as we arrive. The presence of an unfamiliar car tells me Lucia is already here.

"It's cute," she announces.

I inwardly sigh. "Cute" is not the word most people want associated with their home, but I know exactly what she means. It's well-kept, but small. If a realtor were to list it, they'd call it "cozy" or "compact." "I'll get your bag. You head inside."

Tempe seems to consider arguing, but when she climbs out of the car and sways, she decides against it and slowly makes her way up the path. I sling her bag over my shoulder, lock the car, and follow. The house is simple. The room on the right side of the hall is mine. The room to the left is spare. I deposit her bag on the floor and gesture to the spare bed, suddenly feeling self-conscious. It's not a lot.

"This is your room."

"Thank God." She collapses onto the bed and closes her eyes. "I'll be out in a second. I just need a minute."

"Okay. The living room is at the end of the hall."

She nods, and I leave her on the bed even though every fiber of my being screams at me to curl up next to her.

I find Lucia in the living room.

"Where's Tempe?" she asks.

"Resting for a moment. She needs it. She was clearly in a lot of pain earlier."

Lucia stretches out on the sofa. "You care about her, don't you?"

"I do." I won't hide it.

"I get it." She props her chin on one hand. "She's an impressive woman. Beautiful, too, with those gorgeous dark eyes and striking cheekbones."

I don't deny it. I have no desire to. Tempe is, indeed, stunning.

"Just make sure you don't push her too hard, too fast,"

she cautions. "You have a tendency to come on a little strong."

I roll my eyes. Dating advice from my tender-hearted baby sister. Exactly what I need. "I'll try my best."

We chat for a while. Eventually, I go check on Tempe and realize she's fast asleep. My heart fills as I gaze at her. She's so unguarded in this moment. I collect a blanket from the closet and drape it over her.

"Sleep well, beautiful."

———

TEMPE

The sky is dark by the time I wake and tread lightly through Mercy's house. I'm embarrassed I fell asleep on his spare bed before he even had time to show me around. I guess I must have needed it. I pass two other rooms that come off the hall. One is Mercy's and the other is a cramped bathroom. At the end of the hall, I enter a living area that serves as living room, kitchen, and dining room all in one. A sofa and two armchairs occupy one corner while the kitchenette is partially separated by a long, narrow counter. A small, round table occupies the third corner, while the one I'm standing in is basically bare. I suppose it serves as a walkway.

Mercy glances up from the sofa, where he's scrolling on his phone. His sister is nowhere to be seen. "Hey." Crinkles form at the corners of his stunning blue eyes as he smiles. My insides flip over. He's an insanely attractive man. "Did you have a nice nap?"

"Sorry I fell asleep." I cover my flaming cheeks. "That never happens to me."

His smile softens. "I think being tired is a pretty normal side effect of pregnancy, especially when you've been

49

through something like you have today." He holds his phone up. "At least, that's what Dr. Google says."

I giggle and there's a twinge in my side, but it's far less painful than what I was feeling earlier. The spots have partially cleared from my vision too. Perhaps exhaustion exacerbated the effects. "Dr. Google knows everything."

"Exactly." He pats the spot beside him. "Join me?"

I settle onto the sofa, close enough that we could easily touch but far enough away that my hormones don't get any crazy ideas. After the scare earlier, I'm feeling abnormally clingy. I don't have any right to cling to Mercy, and I need to remember that.

"How are you doing?" he asks.

"A little better," I pause, trying to decide how to proceed.

"What's up?" he asks, a line forming between his brows.

I bite my lip. My heart is going crazy, but I know the decision I've arrived at is the right one and I need to share it with him immediately. "I've realized how much I want our baby, even if the timing isn't great." I watch to see his reaction. He relaxes. Encouraged, I continue, "I was scared of being one of those women who's on the verge of having a kickass career only to get pregnant and give it up. My mom was training to be a doctor before she had my sister. She dropped out of medical school to raise us, and I know she always regretted it." I never understood why she didn't go back, but the whole concept just seemed too overwhelming for her. "I didn't want to have regrets and saddle our baby with them, but now I know I'll have just as many if I give her up."

Mercy slides his hand across the space between us and grasps mine. "Thank you for opening up to me. It helps to know where you're coming from." He leans closer and his black hair flops rakishly across his forehead. My pulse skips in response. "I want our baby too, and I'll do whatever I can to make sure you can still have a career and be a mom."

Tears well in my eyes, and I blink furiously, hoping he won't notice. He bundles me into his arms.

"I'm terrified," I admit. "I have no idea what I'm doing."

"Everything will be okay," he murmurs. "We'll figure it out together."

I draw back and study the planes of his handsome face. As always, the sight of him stirs something in me. I don't have the energy to resist the pull between us, so I touch my lips to his. The kiss is tender and only lasts for a few seconds before we separate.

He tucks me against his chest. "I've got you."

I almost want to laugh at how rapidly the situation has turned around. A few days ago, he was the one who needed help while I had my shit sorted. Now, he seems to have fallen into the role of caretaker like he was born into it. "How are you managing this so well?"

He shrugs. "There's not much point in falling apart. You need me." He kisses my forehead. "I'm going to cook some dinner, and then how about we watch a movie?"

I frown, noticing he's changed the subject, but I don't push. We're both stretched thin at the moment and he doesn't need me getting in his face. "That sounds perfect."

Chapter Seven

I reach for the warm body I fell asleep with, but it's nowhere to be found. I blink and open my eyes to gaze at the empty bed. I don't recall coming to the bedroom. My last memory is of resting my head on Mercy's shoulder while the comedy film we'd chosen played in the background. I must have drifted off. Scanning my surroundings, I see my phone on the nightstand and grab it to check the time. It's after nine in the morning. Panic shoots through me. I'm running late to training. I bolt upright, but then I remember. No more training. Not for twelve weeks.

I sigh. What am I going to do with myself until then? MMA is my life. I don't know how else to fill my time. Perhaps I should read some of those books Ashlin recommended about parenthood. I'm going to be a mother, after all. But honestly, reading isn't my thing. I much prefer podcasts and audiobooks. I slide my legs off the edge of the bed and test them to see if they'll take my weight. I'm expecting to be a bit shaky after yesterday, but they seem okay. Standing, I look down at myself. I'm still wearing yoga pants and a tank top. I need to have a shower and change into something fresh, but food comes first. Baby wants yogurt.

I leave the spare room and peek into Mercy's bedroom. The curtains are open and the bed is made, but he's not in it. I linger in the hallway, just out of sight of the living area, to see if I can hear anything. It's quiet, so I head through.

"Good morning."

My gaze snaps to Lucia, who's sitting at the dining table behind a laptop. "Hi. Has Mercy left?"

She nods. "He had to go to work, but he said to help yourself to whatever you need. And apparently, I'm to keep a very close eye on you."

I laugh. "You'll be pleased to know I'm feeling much better today, so I don't think you need to worry. I'm not completely fine, but the blood pressure medication seems to be helping."

"Good." Her eyes lower to my belly. "I want my niece or nephew to be healthy. Do we know which it is?"

"No. I want the gender to be a surprise." I head to the kitchenette and search the refrigerator for yogurt, berries, and milk to make a smoothie. I add them to the blender that's sitting on the counter and pause. "Where's the salt?"

Lucia gestures toward a cupboard tucked into the corner. I grab the salt—which I've been craving—and then pause, remembering I'm not supposed to have too much sodium because it's bad for blood pressure. I set it aside and start the blender, taking a moment to study Lucia while it churns. I didn't pay a lot of attention to her yesterday. I was in too much pain. But her resemblance to Mercy is obvious. She has the same dark hair, although hers is long and straight, and her eyes are a nearly identical shade of blue. Where Mercy is tall and broad-shouldered, Lucia is shorter and curvaceous. She's around my age. Perhaps a couple of years older. I briefly wonder if she begrudges me for getting pregnant with her brother. I couldn't blame her if she did. Mercy is a good guy. He deserves better than to be tied to some girl he had a one-night stand with. But then, our situation isn't my fault any more than it's his. And to be honest, I'm starting to think of it less as a "situation" and more as a blessing in disguise. We've created a life, and that's pretty amazing.

I switch off the blender and pour my smoothie into a glass. "So, Mercy mentioned you work from home. What do you do?"

She glances up from her laptop. "I'm a freelance writer. Most of my money comes from writing articles for magazines, but I've been working on a novel for the past few months. I just can't get the ending right."

My jaw drops. "You're writing a book? That's awesome. What type?"

She blushes. "It's a romance."

Ah, so she's a romantic. "That sounds like a lot of fun."

Her nose wrinkles. "It'd be more fun if I could figure out how to end it."

I round the counter and sit on one of the chairs. "Doesn't there have to be a happily ever after?"

"Yeah, but how do I get them there? That's the problem. I did such a good job of tearing the characters apart that I can't figure out how to put them back together."

"Sorry, that's not ideal." I don't offer any suggestions because I have no freaking idea how to write a romance novel.

"Tell me about it," she huffs, then looks at me as I drink my smoothie. "So, what do you think of my brother?"

I barely manage not to spray my drink across the table. I splutter, then gulp it down. "What do you mean?"

She cocks her head and gives me a look. "I know how

gorgeous he is. All my friends drool over him, and he has a massive heart. I hope you won't break it."

I stare at her for a long moment, unsure how to reply. Finally, I figure I have to say something. "I don't want to hurt him. It's not as though I know him very well, but I like what I do know." I consider my next words carefully. "We've decided not to put the baby up for adoption, so we're going to see a lot more of each other. It's probably stupid to start anything with him, but every time I see him, I want to kiss him. I can't seem to turn it off."

Her eyes sparkle. "If you want to explore something with him, then do it. I'd love to see him settled, but make sure it's what you really want first. He's softer than he seems." Her expression turns wistful. "He had to be a surrogate parent after our mom and dad died in a car accident." I must look shocked because she raises a brow. "He hasn't told you?"

"No," I murmur, wondering what else he hasn't told me.

"It changed his whole life." She pivots her chair to face me better. "He was nineteen. I was twelve. He was in his first year of college, studying business, but he dropped out to take care of me. Sometimes, I think it was too much to ask of him when he was practically a kid himself, but I'm selfishly glad he didn't let me go into the system."

"Wow." I'm quiet while I process the information. "That must have been hard on both of you."

"Yeah." She tilts her head in thought. "Especially for him. I was a preteen girl with an attitude problem. I didn't make it easy. But he was the rock I needed. Steady, loving, strong. He never gave me any hint of how terrified he must have been." She meets my eyes. "My brother is an incredible man. If you make him happy, I'll be grateful to you forever."

I can barely speak. There's a whirlwind of uncomfortable emotion tearing through me. Life must have been difficult for nineteen-year-old Mercy, finding himself the sole guardian of his sister and having his life turned upside down. But look what he made of himself. He learned to tattoo and opened his own parlor. He raised a kind, intelligent woman. Even though he isn't here, I can sense myself losing a piece of my heart to him.

"I'll do my best," I promise, my voice thick. "I just hope he doesn't grow to resent me for the choices I've made."

Lucia smiles. "He won't. He isn't that kind of man."

The shrill ringing of my phone shatters the moment. I reach for it and, seeing it's Dr. Lang, I accept the call.

"Hello?"

"Hi, Tempe." Her tone is brisk but warm. "How are you doing today?"

"Better, but not completely fine."

"You can probably expect to feel that way for the remainder of the pregnancy," she says. "We've got the results back, and they confirm that there's protein in your urine, which supports the diagnosis of preeclampsia."

"Oh." My mood deflates. I've pretty much accepted something is seriously wrong, but having it confirmed forces me to face reality. "Okay, so what happens next?"

"Let's book you in for another appointment this week so we can go over the details. How does tomorrow sound?"

"That should be fine." We set a time and then say our goodbyes.

When I hang up, Lucia slides over next to me and puts an arm around my shoulder. "It's going to be okay," she says. "Mercy and I are both here for you, and we won't let anything go wrong."

I release a shuddering breath, moved by her words. "Thank you."

I can handle this, I remind myself. *It's just like any other fight. Except this time, I can't hit my opponent.*

"Breathe in, and out, out, out."

Tempe and I mimic the woman sitting cross-legged at the front of the room. It's our first birthing class. The instructor is a doula and she's not afraid to tell stories about pregnancies and labors she's been involved in—leaving out people's names, of course. Her stories unnerve me, so I can't imagine how Tempe is feeling. You wouldn't know anything is off to look at her, though. Perhaps it's the result of years of MMA, but she has a killer game face. She looks completely calm and focused.

"Let's shift positions now that you've got the breathing right," the instructor says. "Ladies, sit in front of your partners. Partners, I want you to support mom-to-be both physically and emotionally."

I open my legs and Tempe slides between them. She rests against my chest, and I drop a kiss on her temple. We've shared a few more kisses since she came to stay with me, but our relationship hasn't progressed further than that. Regardless, I already feel like she's mine. We've talked a lot about our hopes and dreams, how we want to raise our child, and what happened in our lives to lead us here. As soon as I opened up to her about raising Lucia, it was like a barrier dropped between us. I feel comfortable with her, and I hope she feels the same.

She nestles closer. "I love when you hold me."

"I wish I could do it all day." Unfortunately, I have to work from dawn until late to earn enough money to pay the bills I owe—and there are many. Finances are the one thing I haven't been completely transparent with her

57

about. Not because it's a secret, but I don't want her to worry. I can fix things; I just need a bit of time.

The teacher walks us through several more exercises and then we head home. It's evening and I can tell Tempe is growing weary. As we walk toward the house, she stops suddenly and grabs my hand, placing it on her stomach. That's when I feel it. A flutter beneath my palm.

"The baby?" I ask.

She nods.

"Wow." I keep my hand there, but they don't kick again. "That's incredible." It's the first time I've felt the baby move, and it's choking me up. A sense of wonder fills me. That's a life we've created together.

"Isn't it amazing?" she asks.

My only answer is to kiss her. I draw her close and revel in the sensation of her nearness. She touches her tongue to mine and presses closer. I skim my hands down her body, and she shivers in response. I deepen the kiss, and soon we're both panting and desperate for more. Memories of our night together flash through my mind. The way she felt, the way she tasted, the way she came apart in my arms. My cock is an iron rod behind my jeans and I groan.

"We have to stop," I remind her. "Remember what the doctor said about sex."

She draws back, scowling. "No vigorous sex."

"Exactly." But seeing the need written across her face, I realize what the doctor didn't say: no orgasms. "I think I have another idea. Come with me." I grab her hand and tug her to the door, where I fumble with the key for a moment before letting us in. I lead her into my bedroom and guide her to the bed. She lies down and rises up on her elbows, clearly trying to figure out what I have in mind. I start to draw down the waistband of her track pants, waiting to see if she'll protest. She doesn't. Until I drop to my knees and she realizes what I'm planning.

"Wait," she says.

I stop and meet her eyes. They're even darker than usual. She's doing nothing to hide her desire. But there's something else there too. Insecurity.

"My stomach is massive and I'm a bit, um, swollen down there."

Huh. I hadn't realized that. "Does it hurt?"

She shakes her head. "It's just sensitive and kinda big."

"I promise I won't think you're anything other than sexy, but if you want me to stop, I will."

She bites her lip and seems to think about it. "If you get turned off, please stop. I'd rather that than anything else."

"I will." I mean it. But I also know there's no way in hell she's going to turn me off. I peel her panties down and can instantly see what she means. The folds of her pussy are puffy, but that only makes me want her more. The sight has me ready to burst.

I lick her before she has time for any doubts. She tastes almost exactly as I remember. I repeat the motion and she whimpers. When I grab her hips to hold her in place, they buck. She's even more sensitive than last time, and it's delightful. I use my tongue and fingers to drive her to the brink. She moans my name as she goes stiff and shudders, then relaxes onto the bed. I give her pussy one last, gentle kiss and slide onto the bed alongside her. My dick is practically screaming for attention, but I ignore it. I wrap my arms around her and kiss her cheek. A few moments later, she's breathing evenly, asleep. I smile, a little smug to have worn her out and helped her get the rest she needs. I stay with her for a while longer, then get up, planning to make myself a hot drink. But something catches my eye. The stack of unpaid bills on the dresser, which I've been making my way through far too slowly.

A shiver creeps up my spine. Fuck, I hate that pile. It

seems unfair I lost so much money and still couldn't save Danny. But the power company and the landlord don't care about my problems, so I'll just have to work even more hours to get them their money. It'll be fine. Everything is under control.

Chapter Eight

TEMPE

Over the next couple of weeks, we fall into a comforting routine. It isn't bad, even though I wish I could be training. I spend my time napping and listening to audiobooks about parenting. I also get online and purchase a few essentials to prepare for the baby, which I store in the corner of the spare room. We haven't decided on future living arrangements yet, and while I've had a look at a few apartments on real estate websites, I haven't found anything that feels right.

Enya and Tony drop by sometimes to watch fight videos and talk strategy. It's great to see Enya. I miss being around her every day. Seth and Ashlin also visit often. Seth and I refine my post-pregnancy game plan, which makes me feel like I have a tenuous grasp of the control that seems to keep slipping out of my grip. Ashlin is a gentle, soothing presence. Sometimes she brings their son, Noah. I haven't had much experience with babies, so it's nice to have the chance to hold him, burp him, and change him with her guidance—all things I'll need to do for my own baby before long. On the few occasions when her visits overlap with Mercy being home, she teaches him to hold and change Noah too.

The one major downside is I see less and less of Mercy. He's gone in the mornings before I wake and doesn't get home until near midnight. I try to nap during the day so I can see him when he walks through the door, but I often fall asleep before he arrives. I've asked him about his work hours because the pace doesn't seem sustainable, but he just says he has a lot of things to get sorted before the baby arrives. Since he isn't willing to share details, I do what I can to ease the burden by preparing his meals—something so domestic I can hardly believe myself—and keeping on top of the housework.

Sometimes, when we're snuggled on the sofa at night, we kiss, and it feels like we're a real couple. Those moments are my favorite. But while we do touch plenty, we never go further. I have a hard time believing he could be attracted to me in my current state. I'm ballooning. And my stomach isn't the only thing that's growing. My ankles keep swelling, and my breasts have gone up a cup size from their pre-pregnancy state.

On a Saturday night, Mercy and I fall asleep together on the sofa while watching a screwball comedy. When I wake, I smile to myself, buoyed by the sensation of a hot, hard man curled around me. I wriggle closer, then freeze. There's something firm pressed against my ass. Something firm, long, and throbbing.

He has an erection.

My pulse picks up. The revelation thrills me. But then my heart sinks. I doubt it's because of me. He probably just has morning wood. Still. Unable to help myself, I rub my booty over the bulge and grin when it thickens in response.

A pair of lips brush the curve of my shoulder to let me

know I'm no longer the only one awake. "Are you having fun?"

His voice is rough from sleep and gives me all kinds of wicked thoughts. I want to hear that harsh tone in my ear as I make him come. But what if he isn't interested in that? Logic tells me men rarely turn down the opportunity to get off, but my insecurities about my pregnant body make me pause.

"Does this happen to you every day?" I ask, hoping the question sounds tongue-in-cheek.

He wraps his arms around me, but not too tight. "Any morning you're around." He nuzzles the crook of my neck. "I'm permanently hard because of you."

"Really?" I don't turn to face him because I'm not sure if I can handle seeing his expression.

"Yes, really." As though sensing I need to hear the words, he adds, "You're the most gorgeous woman I've ever been with. All I can think about is that night we spent together. Pregnant or not, it makes no difference to me. I want you."

My lips tug up at the corners. I awkwardly maneuver myself so I'm facing him. We barely fit on the sofa together, but with how many evenings we've lain here, we've had practice at making it work. I reach between us and undo his zipper, then push his jeans down and rub my palm over his length.

He groans. "Just like that."

I circle his cock with my fingers and pump. He's silky smooth and I wish I could see more, but I'll have plenty of time to explore him later. For now, I just want to make him feel good. I press the pad of my thumb to his slit. Precum is gathered there, and I rub it over the head. He shudders. His pale eyes lock on mine, and the fierce desire in them practically singes me.

"Maybe I should stop," I tease. "Are you sure this is what you want?"

His jaw tightens. "Don't you dare."

I wink and set about jacking him off in earnest. He thrusts into my fist and holds my gaze as his breaths grow shallower and his dick harder. Dampness floods my panties. I squeeze my thighs together and gasp. He tries to cup my crotch, but I bat his hand away. This is all for him. I kiss him, and his mouth immediately opens, our tongues tangling. From his fevered breathing, I can tell he's close to the edge. Using my other hand, I fondle his balls and pick up the pace. His body tenses and his eyes turn to strips of blue that burn into me. Seconds later, he groans and finds his release.

I press a soft kiss to his lips. He returns it and the tenderness in his gaze rocks me. He looks at me as though I'm something precious. Something he adores beyond measure. A couple of tears squeeze out the corners of my eyes.

I'm done for.

Being with Mercy like this is more intense than going all the way with Chad ever was. He tugs off his shirt and uses it to wipe my hand clean, then gathers me against him.

"You're amazing," he murmurs.

"Back at you." I'm beginning to think it wasn't random chance that brought me to Mercy at the bar that night. We're supposed to be together. I only hope nothing goes wrong, because I've been hurt enough.

———

MERCY

I'm dead on my feet from working so much, but I'm also happier than I've been in a long time. Tempe and I might not have chosen for this to happen, but our relationship feels like the real deal. We've been kissing and exchanging orgasms for a few weeks now, and every time I see her, I feel giddy. I haven't been so wrapped up in a woman since I was a teenager. I park outside the house and jog to the front door, energized by the prospect of being with her. She might be asleep by now—she's drifting off earlier and earlier—but I'm eager to see her either way. There's something peaceful about watching Tempe sleep with her hands resting on her belly. It's as though I'm looking into our future.

I try the handle but it's locked, so I slip the key in. I ease the handle down and sneak into the hall. Both bedroom doors are ajar, and the rooms appear empty, although I notice a kitset stroller in a box leaning against the wall. I smile, studying the collection of baby things Tempe has slowly been accumulating. I love the thought that she's fully committed to our child. I've been meaning to suggest she move into my room and we turn the spare into a nursery, but I haven't found the right moment to raise it with her.

As I pass the bathroom, I hear the shower, and my smile widens. I'll have to hurry to let Lucia know I'm home and then join Tempe. I love washing her and letting my hands linger all over her gorgeous body.

I enter the living area. "Hey, Luce."

She glances up from her spot at the table and flashes a smile. "Big day at work?"

"Yeah. I had a couple of unexpected clients turn up late in the day." There had been a time when I'd have turned away anyone presumptuous enough to arrive without an appointment, but for now, I need the extra money, and I don't feel guilty charging them a premium.

"There's chicken fried rice in the fridge for you. Tempe has been cooking."

"Yum." I head into the kitchen, and a letter on the counter catches my eye. My good mood evaporates. It's from the landlord. I tear it open and withdraw the paper, hoping my actions are casual enough not to draw Lucia's attention. The header reads *Rent Due: Final Notice*.

My heart sinks. I skim the text. The letter is to advise me I have two weeks to pay off all rent owing or the landlord will send a formal eviction notice. I can't even be angry at him. I've paid off a little of the balance, but nowhere near all of it. I get on with him well, so I thought I'd have more time, and I've been focusing on reducing the balance I owe for utilities and medical bills instead. It seems I shouldn't have done that. I squeeze my eyes shut and rub my temples. I guess I'll have to book more clients this week. Perhaps if I work through the weekend, I'll be able to pay enough rent to get him off my back until I can gather the rest of what I owe.

"Mercy."

I freeze. It's Tempe's voice. She's standing in the doorway between the hall and the living area. Her brow is furrowed with concern.

"What's wrong?"

I open my mouth to tell her everything. I want to spill it all. How I lost my money trying to save Danny and have been on the back foot ever since. Not even Lucia knows about my precarious financial situation. I want to warn Tempe we might need to find somewhere else to live. She doesn't have her apartment anymore. She's already canceled the lease and moved the last of her belongings over. But as I open my mouth to speak, Tempe winces and rubs her side.

I stop. I can't unload everything on her. She's already unwell, and we were specifically told to keep her stress down. If I burden her with something I should be able to fix myself, it might harm her or the baby. I can't do that.

However much I might want to share the load, I need to protect her. I care for her too much to risk her health. Besides, I've been in crappy situations before and found my way out. It's not as though it was easy trying to raise my twelve-year-old sister when I was a teenager myself. My jaw sets. I've been through worse. I can manage. There's no need to worry her. I tuck the letter into my back pocket and force a grin.

"I have a headache. Don't think I drank enough today."

"Oh." She pads over and kisses my cheek. "You do feel a little warm. Let me get you some water and a Tylenol."

Guilt churns in my stomach. I just lied to her for the first time, and I fucking hate it. But what else am I supposed to do? Put her in harm's way because I was stupid enough to get myself into debt? I refuse to do that.

She fills a clean glass with water and passes it to me. "Here you go. Hang on a sec and I'll grab a tablet."

"Don't worry about that." I snag her fingers and squeeze them reassuringly. "Water is all I need."

Behind her, Lucia gives me a strange look. She can see through my act. Fortunately, she doesn't say a word. Tempe waits for me to finish drinking, then takes the empty glass from me and sets it on the counter. She wraps her arms around me and rests her head on my chest.

"I missed you today."

"I missed you too," I murmur. It's the truth, and yet I feel like a fraud. What the hell am I supposed to do next?

Chapter Nine

TEMPE

I run a cloth across the top of the nightstand next to Mercy's bed. There's hardly any dust on the surface, but I've already put together the kitset stroller I bought online, and I'm eager to do anything even remotely useful. I've never spent so much time off my feet in my life. I go to the dresser and dust off the end that's clear, then gather the pile of letters from the other end to wipe the wood beneath them, but when I catch sight of the header on the top letter, everything inside me goes still. It's a demand for overdue rent. But surely, that can't be right. Mercy isn't the type of guy to default on rent, and with how much he's been working, he must have the money—or at least some of it.

I finger the edge of the letter. I should put it away and mind my own business. It's addressed to him, and I'm pretty sure it's illegal to open someone else's mail. But then, it's already open, and it kind of *is* my business if I'm going to need to find a new place to live sooner rather than later. I grip the edge of the letter and slide it out of the envelope. The floor creaks and I slap a hand to my chest, frightened.

"Get a grip," I mutter to myself. "It's just your imagination."

I scan the letter, feeling worse and worse with each sentence. Mercy really has defaulted on the rent payments. According to this, he's several months overdue. Nausea churns in my gut. How can that be possible? Does he have a secret gambling addiction or drug problem that sucks up all of his money?

No, I tell myself. *I'd know if he was on drugs.*

But gambling? I'd like to think not, but the man I believed him to be wouldn't hide the possibility of eviction, so how well do I really know him? Perhaps all those hours he's away, he isn't working. Maybe he's at the casinos. There are certainly enough places in Vegas to gamble away rent money.

I slip the letter back inside the envelope and, on impulse, flick through the other letters. My heart sinks further when I see logos for the electric company and the internet provider. But it's the final few letters that make me pause. They're from a hospital and a funeral home. I place the letters back on the dresser, disappointed in myself for having looked. Whatever is going on with his finances, I shouldn't find out by snooping through his things. I'll just ask him when he gets home.

I sit on the edge of the bed and draw in a slow breath. Mercy has clearly omitted to tell me some very important facts. He might not have outright lied, but he should have clued me in to the situation. When it has the potential to affect our baby, I deserve to know. And honestly, I'm a bit hurt he wouldn't confide in me, given the direction our relationship is taking. I've been trying to get him to open up ever since I moved in, but the man is like a brick wall. He wants to hear all of my worries but rarely shares his.

Lights dance in front of my eyes, and I realize my breathing has become shallow. I try to haul in a deeper breath, but my lungs protest. Head swimming, I lie down, struggling to find a position that's comfortable. I breathe in for the count of six and slowly exhale, then repeat. The wooziness decreases, but I still don't feel well enough to stand.

"Lucia!" I call, hoping she hasn't got her headphones plugged in, so she'll be able to hear me.

A few seconds later, she appears above me, haloed by the ceiling lights. "Are you okay?" She sounds panicked. "What happened? Do you need the doctor?"

"I'm okay," I assure her. "I think I've overdone it. Would you be able to bring me a glass of water?"

"Sure thing." She sinks onto the bed beside me and touches my forehead. "You feel clammy. Are you certain you don't need a doctor?"

"Pretty sure. But I'll let you know if I start feeling worse."

"You'd better." She narrows her eyes at me like she's teasing, but her voice is serious.

I smile weakly. "Promise."

She nods and heads to the door. "Be back in a moment."

I grab my phone and turn on a calming meditation soundtrack. I've never had much patience for meditation, but when forced to do it, I find it easier with music to concentrate on. When Lucia returns, she helps me drink, then pulls the blankets over me.

"Be safe."

She leaves me alone with nothing but my thoughts and the music for company. It feels like forever before Mercy finally comes home.

———

I pull off my nitrile gloves and stretch my hands above my head. I've been hunched over a client for the better part of four hours. Thankfully, the image on his back is finally starting to take shape. He probably only needs one more session to complete it.

"How are you feeling?" I ask. This particular client has had several other tattoos, so I trust him to evaluate how his body is reacting. The process of getting inked can be physically stressful for some people and induce highs for others.

"Not too bad." He sits up and reaches for his shirt so he can gingerly slip it back on. I've covered the tattoo temporarily. Once he's home, he can remove the covering if needed.

I pull my phone from my pocket and check the calendar. "Don't forget to clean it and apply the lotion. I've got you booked in for four weeks' time to put the finishing touches on." I hesitate, then add, "There's a chance I'll have to reschedule because I'm expecting a baby around then, but I'll keep you up to date."

My client grins and sticks out a hand for me to shake. "Congratulations, man. Kids are such a blessing."

"Thanks." I smile back. "I've kinda done the dad thing before with my sister, but she was far from a newborn, so I'm not sure what to expect."

"A lot of crying and dirty diapers," he jokes. "Nah, babies are pretty incredible. You're a smart guy; you'll figure it out."

"I hope so." I watch him lumber toward the desk to pay. "See you next time."

"Good luck."

I glance down at my phone again and notice I have a message from Lucia.

Lucia: *Tempe isn't feeling well. She looks uncomfortable but I don't think she's bad enough to call a doctor.*

Nerves knot in my stomach. Lucia wouldn't mention something like that unless she was legitimately concerned. Damn. I have one more client before I can go home, and I'd hate to cancel when I need all the money I can get.

Mercy: *Are you sure? Should I come home early?*

Lucia: *No, we'll be fine. I didn't mean to worry you. Just wanted you to know.*

I huff in frustration. I should go home. I want to. The need to see Tempe and make sure she's okay thrums in my veins, but I have to trust Lucia if she says things aren't bad enough to justify me leaving.

The next two hours are the slowest of my life. By the time I manage to usher my final client out the door, every cell in my body is screaming at me to get to Tempe. I lock up and speed back to the house. I race up to the doorstep and open it, just as Lucia steps into the hall. She glances behind herself and closes the door.

"Is she okay?" I demand.

Lucia moves closer. "You need to talk to her," she murmurs. "Something is wrong, but I don't think it's completely to do with her health. She won't say anything to me. I've been asking about it all evening."

I nod. "Okay, thanks." I kiss her cheek. "See you tomorrow?"

"Bright and early. Good luck."

Her parting words send a shiver of premonition down my spine. Something tells me I won't enjoy whatever conversation I'm about to have.

"Thanks." I haul in a lungful of oxygen and stride to the living area. Tempe is curled on the sofa. She looks at me in a way that makes me cold. As though she doesn't recognize me.

"Did you have a good day at work?" Her question is stilted.

"It was okay. Long." I try to kiss her, but she flinches away. "What's wrong?"

She drops her feet to the floor and straightens, as though pulling herself together. The motion makes me nervous. "Tell me about the stack of bills in your bedroom."

No.

I close my eyes. Of course she found them. It was only a matter of time. Judging from her demeanor, I have some explaining to do, and I'd better get started fast.

"It's going to be okay. I'm a bit behind on some of my payments, but I'll find a way to make it work. I'll still be able to support you and the baby. I've almost caught up on the utilities bills, but I thought the landlord would give me more time."

She crosses her arms and glares. "This isn't about the money. It's about you not being open with me so we could solve the problem together."

I stiffen. "It's my problem, not yours. I didn't want to burden you with it and add to your stress. Your health and our baby's health are important to me. I've been working extra hours to make sure I can pay everything I owe."

She sighs in exasperation. "It's *our* problem because we're supposed to be a team. If we're in a relationship—or whatever the hell this is—then we should be equals within it. You can't coddle me. I'm not your baby sister, I'm your partner. When you don't treat me that way, it hurts."

Her words slip between my ribs like a knife and plunge into my heart. "I'm sorry." I take her hand, relieved she doesn't pull away this time. I couldn't stand it if she did. She's grown to mean the world to me, and I can't lose her. "I love you. I'm sorry I didn't tell you about the bills. It's just that I'm so close to having everything I want, and I'm afraid I'm going to lose it. Lose *you*."

Her lips part and her eyes widen. I've shocked her. Of

course I have. I shouldn't have blurted it all out like that. But her expression softens. Not enough to soothe me, but enough to give me hope.

"I love you too, Mercy, but it's not okay for you to hold things back like this. It makes me wonder how well we really know each other." She presses her lips together and when I see them tremble, it makes me feel like the lowest form of scum. "This has all happened so fast. I've been in a relationship before where I wasn't treated as an equal and I won't do it again. If we're going to make this work, something needs to change."

"It will," I promise, my heart threatening to break at the sound of the pain in her words. I never meant to make her feel this way. I just wanted to take care of things so she wouldn't have to, like I've been doing for everyone else my whole damn life. But she's right. I haven't treated her as a partner. I should have trusted her to be strong enough to handle it. "Can I tell you something?"

"Yes." She squeezes my hand, and in this moment, I feel utterly unworthy of her. She'd be well within her rights to yell and scream and storm out, but instead, she's giving me the chance to talk. To finally be honest about the mess my life has become. "I want to listen."

"Thank you," I whisper. I close my eyes and think back to eighteen months ago, when I first noticed something was wrong with Danny. "There was a guy who worked for me and became my friend. He started spending a lot of time on sick leave. I got worried and went to check on him one day. He was in a really bad state but didn't want to see a doctor. I think he suspected what was wrong, and he was scared and broke. He was using almost all his money to pay for his elderly mother's care and refused to do anything to jeopardize that. So I paid for him to see a doctor. He got referred to a specialist to have some procedures done before they could confirm what was wrong."

"And you paid for all of it?" Tempe asks.

"I did. He argued, but I said I could afford it. Then they told us he had cancer. It was bad, but there was a chance he'd survive with chemo. He didn't have the money, so I insisted on paying." I let out a shaky breath, remembering how Danny had fought with me over it. He'd been so weak, and I couldn't handle not doing whatever I could to help. We'd been friends for years.

"For a while, it was okay. But then he didn't get better. My savings ran out. I couldn't give up on him, so I put all of the money I could spare toward his care. It still wasn't enough, so I took out a medical loan. I never let him know how tight things were. I knew he'd tell me to stop, but I couldn't just let him die." I bury my face in my hands. I've cried plenty of tears for Danny, but when I think about those last few weeks of his life, my eyes still prickle with emotion.

"They tried to save him, but there was nothing they could do. The cancer had spread throughout his body. When he died, what little he had left went to his mom, to continue her care. I knew how important that was to him, and I didn't want the funeral costs whittling away at the estate, so I paid for his funeral too. I knew I'd be able to make the money back eventually, with how well the tattoo parlor does. It's just taking longer than I thought." Finally, I run out of words. I raise my eyes to look at her, afraid this will be the part where she sees what a mess I am and leaves.

Instead, she slides closer and wraps an arm around my shoulders. "I'm sorry you lost him. I've never been through something like that, but it must have been awful."

"Yeah," I say hoarsely. "I watched him waste away a bit more every day."

She smooths a hand down my back. "Thank you for telling me."

I study her beautiful face. "What do we do now?"

"To start with, you let out all that emotion you've been holding in. Yell, cry, hit things—whatever it takes. When you're done, I'll reheat dinner and we can discuss our next steps. Okay?"

She's not leaving?

All I can do is nod. I'll agree to anything that doesn't result in her walking through the exit for good.

Chapter Ten

My hands tremble as I serve a portion of vegetable bake onto a plate and find a set of cutlery to accompany it. There's a hollow ache in my chest that won't go away. I keep thinking about how Mercy must have felt watching his friend slowly succumb to cancer while he sunk further into debt trying to save him. Mercy is such a natural care-taker that I can imagine how it played out. No wonder he's so protective of me. But whatever his reasons, it wasn't right of him to hide the situation. I bite my lip, anxious about the conversation to come. I know it won't be easy, but I have to stand my ground if we want to have any chance of coming out the other side of this as a functional couple.

"Here." Mercy has shifted to the table, and I set the plate in front of him.

He glances up at me but doesn't smile. I can tell he's waiting for me to pull the rug out from under him. "Thank you. It smells great."

I nod in acknowledgment, then head to his bedroom

77

and grab the bills from his dresser. When I return, he tenses.

"I need to know exactly how much you owe, and to whom," I tell him. "We'll work through these while you eat."

"Okay." To my surprise, he agrees without any fuss.

For the next half hour, we go through his bills, discarding the ones he's paid and marking the ones that are most urgent—with rent at the top of the list. Several times, I have to pause and take a few slow and steady breaths to get my pulse under control. I don't want anything to happen to me, or it will make Mercy believe he was right to keep secrets.

"So, what now?" he asks as he pushes his empty plate aside and eyes the bills that remain on the table. The ones yet to be paid. I have to admit, he's done a good job of catching up in the past couple of months, but he has a reasonable way to go.

I place my palms on my thighs and grip firmly, knowing he won't like what I'm about to suggest. "I have enough savings to pay off everything you owe. Chad liked to support me financially because it inflated his ego. It annoyed me at the time, but I have a healthy savings account, so I guess I should be grateful. I could make it all go away, and I'd still have enough left to cover any emergencies."

"No," he says flatly. "Not going to happen."

I purse my lips. Damn stubborn man. "Look, you might think you're an island, but this affects me too. I know you're used to being the one who gives, not the one who receives, but in a healthy relationship, it goes both ways." I can see from his expression I'm getting to him, so I soldier on. "It would be a weight off my mind to be able to wipe the slate clean, so we don't have any debt to worry about going forward."

He digs a thumb into his jaw, just beneath his ear. "It doesn't feel right to take your savings when it's my poor money management that got me into this mess."

I brush my foot against his beneath the table. "We're a team. I'll remind you of that as many times as it takes. You have to be able to lean on me sometimes, or this will never work. Anyway, if we're going to have a real relationship, perhaps I could stay here with you rather than finding my own place, in which case it would be only right that I contribute."

He's silent for a moment. I can practically hear the whir of his brain as he thinks through his options. I scarcely dare to breathe, I'm so nervous to see how he responds. Our future rides on this. Finally, he offers me a tiny smile. "Okay. That would be incredible." He looks down at his hands, then seems to force himself to meet my eyes. "Thank you for staying with me and for being such an amazing partner. I promise, I'm going to do better at sharing in the future, if you'll give me a chance."

I open my mouth to assure him I'm willing to work things out, but a rush of liquid soaks my underwear and the crotch of my yoga pants. "Uh-oh."

———

Mercy

"Uh-oh?" I ask. That's not the reply I'd been hoping for. I reach for her hand, ready to beg and plead, but then I catch sight of her expression. Her mouth is frozen, and she's turning pale. "What is it?"

She clutches her hand to her chest. "I think my water just broke. Either that or I peed myself."

"Shit." I lurch out of my chair and hurry around to help her. "The baby isn't due for a month."

"I know." She looks as panicked as I feel. "I'll give you

all the chances you want if you call Dr. Lang right now and get me to the hospital."

I nod, and then nod some more as I fumble my phone from my pocket because fucking hell, the baby might be coming. I call Dr. Lang's number. Fortunately, she's on shift. She sounds concerned when I update her on what's happened, and I try not to read into it, but I've never been so scared in my life. Not even when I held Danny's hand as he took his last breaths. I shove the phone back into my pocket and run my fingers through my hair. What do we need? The bag we've packed, just in case. What the hell else did the birthing teacher say?

A sudden gasp draws me from my thoughts. Tempe is clutching her stomach, her face twisted in pain.

"Are you okay?" I touch her arm. She must be having a contraction. "Breathe through it. You've got this."

She groans. "We need to go."

"But what about—"

"Get the car!" she yells. "I don't care about anything else. Just get me to the damn hospital. This baby is coming early."

I grab the bag, snatch my keys from the kitchen counter and put an arm around her as I escort her to the door. I lock up behind us, hoping against hope I haven't forgotten anything important. She sits in the back, and I shove the bag in the trunk and start the engine. The drive to the hospital seems to take forever. Several more contractions hit her, and all I can do is put my foot harder on the accelerator.

"It's okay, sweetheart," I soothe as her breathing picks up. She needs to keep her blood pressure as low as possible or things will get worse. "Take some deep breaths. Imagine you're at a fight. Round one has finished, and you have a minute before round two starts. You need to get your breathing under control. I know you can do it."

80

I pull up outside the hospital's front entrance.

"Stay here. I'll only be a second." I race up the ramp and inside, where I speak to a nurse. She finds a wheelchair and accompanies me to get Tempe. "Go with the nurse," I tell her. "I'll park the car and be right behind you."

"Please hurry." She climbs out of the back seat and gets into the wheelchair without argument. She must be feeling really bad.

"I will." While the nurse wheels her inside, I drive in circles around the parking garage, cursing until I find a space. I switch off the car and race for the entrance. I don't pause at reception but hurry straight to Doctor Lang's department. When I get there, the woman at the desk waves me along the corridor. I glance into every open room until I arrive at the one with Tempe in it. The doctor has positioned her on the bed, and her lower half has been stripped, except for a blanket draped over her legs.

"Is everything okay?" I ask.

Dr. Lang is standing between Tempe's legs, peering beneath the blanket. "The baby wants to be born," she says. "It's early, but not early enough to make me worry about there being significant developmental problems. He or she has a good chance of being completely healthy. We just need to get Tempe through the labor."

She checks a screen. "Her blood pressure is very high. We'll need to give her medication to keep it down during the birth, but not so much that she gets sleepy or that it risks injury to the baby." She turns to a nurse, who has been busy connecting something to the back of Tempe's hand. "Good to go?" The nurse nods. "Deliver the dose." Dr. Lang glances at Tempe's face. "We're going to manage this the best we can, but I need you to push hard when the time comes. The faster your baby is born, the less likely anything will go wrong with their blood supply. Okay?"

Tempe nods wearily. A moment later, her face screws

up as she experiences another contraction. I drag a chair to the side of the bed opposite the medical personnel and take her hand. She squeezes so tightly I wince, but whatever she does to me, I know it has nothing on what she's going through. I wish I could take the pain for her, but I'll have to settle for giving her whatever support she needs.

Hours pass, but time seems to move in a vacuum. The contractions come more quickly, and then, all of a sudden, Tempe screams. It's the most awful sound I've ever heard.

"I've got you," I whisper. "You can do this. You're a fighter."

The doctor orders her to push. Tempe's forehead is slicked with sweat and her lips are twisted in agony, but she does. My warrior woman summons a depth of strength I've never witnessed as she brings our baby into this world. I'm blown away by her. How could I ever have thought she needed me to shelter her from adversity? She can do anything. There's no way I'd be so courageous in her shoes. All I can do is stay with her, let her crush my hand, and murmur encouragement while she goes through something the likes of which I never will.

When our baby emerges, I hold my breath for the two seconds it takes them to start crying.

"You did it," I tell her. "The baby is okay."

Tempe goes limp, panting as she tries to look down at our child.

Dr. Lang passes the baby to a nurse, who gently dries them. "Mercy, would you like to cut the cord?"

"Yes, please." I'm surprised to hear the tremble in my voice. She makes preparations, and I take the sterilized blade from her and carefully cut through the umbilical cord. I pass the blade back, and Dr. Lang takes care of the rest. I wish I could see more of what's happening, but I stay where I am so Tempe and I will get to properly meet our baby at the same time.

Dr. Lang does a quick physical check and smiles. "Congratulations! You have a baby girl."

"A girl," I whisper, meeting Tempe's eyes. Love swells within me for both her and our newborn. It's so powerful a couple of tears slip down my cheeks. "We have a daughter."

Even though she's clearly hurting, Tempe's smile is radiant. "Can I hold her?"

"Of course." Dr. Lang bundles the tiny infant in a blanket. "Now, Daddy, you might need to help Mommy at first. She'll be tired after all the work she's done, and her muscles may be fatigued."

I nod, and when she gently passes our daughter, still crying, to Tempe, I lean closer to help support her weight. I stare at our daughter's face, utterly entranced. She has a little button nose, pale brown skin, and a few tufts of black hair. I stroke the top of her head. Her hair is so soft. Her skin too. She's delicate.

Tempe cradles the baby to her chest, resting against the pillows, and the cries fade away. "Hi, little one. I'm your mommy, and this is your daddy." Our eyes meet, and the emotion in hers nearly fells me. I understand it, though, because I feel it too. "She's beautiful."

"She is," I agree. "Our baby."

Tempe's breath catches. "You're perfect." She looks down at the baby again, her expression filled with love. "Welcome to our family."

Warmth envelops me. *Our family*. It sounds like everything I've ever wanted. I can't take my eyes off my baby girl and the woman I will treasure every day for the rest of my life.

"I love you already," I tell our daughter. "We both do. Forever and ever."

Epilogue

Tony

"You can do this," I mutter to myself as I stand outside the hospital room. "You like babies."

It's true. I love babies. But they scare me when they belong to one of my friends because it's yet another sign I'm reaching the stage in life where people expect me to settle down and have kids. But that isn't my plan. The thought of being responsible for another person terrifies me.

"You going in?" I jolt at the voice behind me and spin around. Vic stands there, smirking like an idiot, witnessing my moment of weakness.

I clear my throat. "Yeah, of course. I was just trying to remember the baby's name."

As excuses go, it's weak. Baby Madison is all anyone's been talking about at the gym.

"Madison," he says. "Come on, tough guy."

I push the door open and step inside. Tempe is propped up in bed, an adorable munchkin cradled to her chest. Mercy sits in the chair beside her, staring at them as though they're his entire world. It's kinda sweet. Not that I'd say so to his face. Let the man keep his pride.

I take a few steps forward so Vic can enter. "Hey, guys. Congratulations."

Tempe smiles. "Thank you."

If I didn't know she'd been blindsided by her pregnancy, I'd never have guessed it. She seems completely content. I pace over to the side of the bed to get a better look at baby Madison, but as I do, someone moves in the corner of my vision. I stop and turn. There's a woman standing to my right, pressed against the wall. All thoughts vacate my head except the need to know her name. She's a goddess, with curves built for sin, silky black hair, and the most stunning blue eyes I've ever seen. Those eyes are almost completely unique. The only person I've met with eyes like that is… *Mercy*.

Shit. My jaw drops. Could this gorgeous creature be his baby sister? I've heard him speak about her.

Lucia.

I want to taste the name on my tongue, but I don't dare. From what Tempe and Enya have said, she's a white picket fence type. She wants a home, a family, and a bright future full of possibilities. I'm not the guy to give her that.

Lucia meets my eyes and sends me the sweetest smile I've ever received. My heart sinks. That sweet smile is the only thing I can ever accept from her. There will be no kisses, no lingering glances. Lucia Caruso is off limits. I can look, but not touch. And as interest flares in her beautiful eyes and her cheeks turn pink, I know staying away might be the hardest thing I'll ever do.

Extended Epilogue - 12 Months Later

MERCY

I watch as Tempe puts her mouth guard in and Seth checks her over. It's her first fight after returning to the gym and my heart is in my throat as she prepares. She looks strong and she's excited, so I'm putting on a good face, but I'm not sure how I'm going to get through this. I turn Madison around in my arms so she can see Tempe.

"That's your mom," I say. "You should be very proud of her. She's the toughest woman I know."

"She is."

I glance at Enya, who's come to stand beside me. We've become friends over the past year. She and her boyfriend, Jimmy, dote on Madison, and she's had to deal with my constant texts to check on Tempe ever since she returned to training. "When's your next fight?"

"Not for a few months. Jimmy has one next weekend, though." She nods toward Tempe. "She's in great shape. She's going to kick butt out there."

"Thanks." I try to remain calm for Madison's sake. "I know she's been working hard." An usher appears in the doorway and gestures for Tempe and the others to move into the hall. It's nearly time for her fight. I grab Tempe by the shoulder and stop her for long enough to kiss her forehead. "Be careful out there. Good luck."

She grins, revealing the rubber of her mouth guard between parted lips. "I won't need luck."

I smile even though my heart is hammering, and back away as she blows me another kiss and heads for the door with Seth, Enya, and Harley. As soon as she's out of view, I lower myself onto a chair and bring up the live stream of the arena on my phone. I'd rather watch her in person, but we agreed it would be better not to expose Madison to the hype of an MMA stadium until she's older.

Tempe's opponent walks into the arena first and enters the cage. A couple of minutes later, Tempe follows. She moves with confidence, reminding me she knows what she's doing. I watch with bated breath while both fighters stand in the center of the ring and the referee speaks to them. Then the first round begins.

Tempe comes out strong. They exchange punches and kicks. Soon, before the timer sounds, Tempe pins her opponent to the edge of the cage and grapples with her. They fall to the floor. I want to squeeze my eyes shut but force myself to look. I need to know what's happening.

"She's got this," I murmur to Madison. "Your mommy is going to be fine."

She doesn't understand, but she gurgles happily, which makes me feel better. The round ends and Seth leaps into the cage. He says something to Tempe while Enya and Harley ice her body. Shortly after, the second round begins. I feel sick when the other fighter lands a kick to Tempe's midsection, but she strikes back, unshaken. They struggle for dominance over the course of the round. By the time it ends, I have no idea who's winning. My heart says Tempe, but I'm a little biased.

In the third round, Tempe's opponent is clearly worn

out. Her strikes are sloppy and her hands are low, allowing Tempe to hit her where it hurts. My woman isn't anywhere near running out of steam, though. She keeps up the same consistent attack and precise movements she has since round one. When the fight ends, I know she's come out on top. It's not just wishful thinking on my part. She did exactly what she'd feared she wouldn't be able to. Returned to the fighting scene with a vengeance. As the referee lifts her hand, my heart feels too big for my chest.

"She did it, Madi." I raise Madison's tiny hand as though she's cheering for her mother. "Yay! Go, Mom!"

We wait for her to come back to us, and it seems to take forever. First, I see Harley, then Seth, and finally, Enya and Tempe, who have their arms wrapped around each other.

"You were awesome out there," I say, passing Madison to Seth so I can gather Tempe in my arms. "Just incredible. I'm so proud of you."

She glows. "I won."

"I know." I kiss her. "You're back in the game."

"We're going to have plenty of other fighters wanting to go up against you," Seth says. "Are you ready for that?"

She and I exchange a glance.

"As ready as I'll ever be," she replies. "As long as I get to go home to my family at the end of the day."

Seth smiles. "I want to go home to mine too, so that's a given. Is the childcare situation still all right?"

I nod. We've set up a playpen in the corner of the tattoo parlor, and someone is with Madison at all times. My staff adore her. They squabble over who gets to play with her. It's honestly been such a gift. We're very lucky.

"Tempe." I reach into my pocket, hoping I'm about to get even luckier. "Madi and I have a question for you."

She grins. "What's that?"

I take Madison from Seth and place the small black

88

box between her chubby palms. Tempe's eyes widen. She glances from the box to me and back again.

"Open it," I whisper.

She takes the box from Madison and carefully pops it open. Inside, a white gold ring is nestled on a black velvet bed. A bunch of tiny diamonds form the shape of a heart. Lucia helped me choose it. I hope it's not too corny.

"It's beautiful," she breathes.

I drop to my knee, holding Madison at my hip. "Temperance Larson, will you marry us?"

"Yes. I will." She sweeps Madison into her arms and whirls her in a circle. Our daughter laughs with delight. Someone claps. Tempe stops spinning and sandwiches Madison between us so she can kiss me slowly. "How did you know I was ready?"

"Because you've finally proven to yourself that you can be a good mom and a successful fighter."

"And a wife," she adds with a wink.

"Congratulations, guys." I'm not sure who says it because I can't take my eyes off my soon-to-be wife. Other people echo the sentiment.

"I love you," I tell Tempe. "I'm so glad fate decided to bring us together."

We've agreed not to call the pregnancy an accident since we never want Madison to believe we don't want her with our whole hearts.

"Me too." Tempe leans closer and whispers, "How soon do you think we can get married?"

———

TEMPE - 3 MONTHS LATER

"Take off your clothes, Mrs. Caruso."

I shiver at Mercy's commanding tone. It's our wedding night. The first night we've been alone and uninterrupted for months. After a small ceremony this afternoon, Seth and Ashlin took Madison to stay with them.

"After you, Mr. Caruso." I slip my dress off to reveal a matching set of white underwear.

A muscle in his jaw ticks. "You're so fucking sexy. And you're all mine."

I waggle my ring finger at him. "That's what this says."

"Good." He drags me into a kiss that's all hot tongues and mingled breath. His hand cups my pussy and he groans. "Can't wait to get inside you."

We've been insatiable since a couple of months after Madison's birth, when we were finally able to have sex properly. Now, we can't get enough of each other.

I smooth my hands down his chest and work on his buttons. I open one after another, slowly exposing more of his tattooed chest and abdomen. When they're all undone, I ease the shirt off over his shoulders. He wraps his arms around me, his body hot against mine, and then he eases down the thin straps of my panties. I lick one of his nipples, enjoying the way he shudders in response. He slicks a finger into my sex and strokes.

"No teasing this first time," I say. "I need you too much. We've got all night to go slow."

He brushes his lips to mine. "Hard and fast, then slow and sweet."

"Exactly."

He releases me and fumbles with his tuxedo pants, kicking them off. My mouth waters. My husband is a sexy man. Tall, lean, but with muscular thighs and an ass I could stare at for days. Tattoos wind down one of his legs as far as the knee, but the other is bare. Apparently he's saving it for the future. I reach inside his boxers and fist his cock.

"Oh fuck." His head falls back. "Yeah, that's it, baby."

I lick my lips as I work his boxers down, and the

plump head of his dick comes into view. The tip is weeping. He's as desperate as I am. Seeing him in this suit all day but being unable to do anything about it has driven me crazy. Mercy's fingers grip my chin and raise my gaze to his.

"Not now," he says. "I won't last."

Pleasure thrums at the top of my thighs. "Then hurry up and fuck me already."

He laughs. "When did you get so impatient?"

"The moment you touched me under the table," I remind him.

"Oh yeah." He looks pleased with himself.

I flick open the clasp of my bra and bare my breasts to him. His eyes darken with need, and any trace of humor vanishes. He grabs me by the hips and carries me to the bed, settling on top of me, his knees between my thighs, keeping them apart. His cock is hard and at full attention. He leans over me, his arms on either side of my head, and notches against my entrance. His hips shift and he rocks in bit by bit. His thumb finds my clit.

"Yes," I whimper. "Again."

He repeats the motion, pumping into me with each stroke. I watch his cock get enveloped by my pussy over and over again. When I finally look up, I find him staring at me, his lips parted, expression hungry. He captures my mouth and swallows my moan. We move together, as close as two people can be, as we climb toward our peak. An orgasm builds within me, and I angle my hips, urgently seeking it out. He slams into me, hitting that bundle of nerves that brings every cell of my body to life.

"Please," I beg. "I need to come."

His hands slide under my back and tilt my body. The new angle shifts me so when he thrusts in, starbursts explode behind my eyes, and I rocket into a world of bliss. He goes stiff above me, and I feel his dick jerk as he finds his release. I close my eyes and hold him tight. "Love you, love you, love you."

We both fall silent as we catch our breath. Then Mercy rises up on his elbows and smooths my hair off my forehead.

"I love you so much, Tempe. It's you and me from here on out."

"And Madison," I add.

"And Madi." He buries his face in the crook of my neck. "You two have made me so happy."

"You've made my life so much bigger than it already was."

We lie together, chest to chest, and it feels like our hearts are beating in sync. All I can think is I want this every day for the rest of my life.

With Mercy by my side, I'll have it.

THE END

Fighter's Heart Excerpt

LENA

Eight words. That's all it takes to ruin my day.

"LaFontaine, I have a special assignment for you."

I recognize the voice without looking up from my desk. It's my prick of a boss, Adrian, and anything he's terming a "special assignment" will inevitably be a nightmare. That's all I get these days. The unfixable cases. The spoiled, self-entitled sports stars who screw up so badly, no one else wants them.

God, one massive win and I become the go-to public relations girl for the biggest jerks-with-abs in Vegas. Why can't I, just once, get a client who's a marginalized feminist with a cause? Sighing, I raise my head and meet Adrian's beady little eyes. This douchebag has my career in his hands, and he knows it.

"What's the case?"

His thin lips curl in a self-satisfied smile. It doesn't escape my notice that he's yet to close the door, which makes me wonder if he's keeping it open as an escape route.

"Jase Rawlins."

Oh. Hell. No.

"Nuh-uh," I say. "No freaking way."

Jase "The Wrangler" Rawlins is one of the bad boys of MMA. I don't even have to ask why he needs our services. Anyone who pays attention to the sports industry knows his ex-girlfriend has come forward with allegations of domestic abuse. I've seen photos of her bruised cheek and read the story in popular magazines. The guy is violent. But I suppose I shouldn't expect any different from a cage fighter.

I know the type. I've *dated* the type.

"There's no way I'm working with that asshole. Absolutely not. Find someone else. I'm not aiding and abetting a jackass who thinks he can get away with hitting women."

The door opens wider, and Jase Rawlins himself steps into my small, airy office, his gaze immediately drawn to the view out the window, which looks over the business district. I know him on sight, and I'm not even sorry he overheard my comment. He deserves all the condemnation he gets, and more. Fuck him.

Adrian's brows draw together, as if he didn't expect me to argue. "Everything is organized, Lena. The papers are signed. It's a done deal."

My teeth scrape together loud enough I'm surprised no one else hears them. I meet Jase's eyes, and a jolt runs through me. They're a strange color. Dark gray, or maybe green, it's hard to tell, and fringed with the thickest lashes I've ever seen. Pretty eyes. Out of place on a man known for choking his opponents into submission. He has high, arrogant cheekbones and plush lips, although the upper one is marred by a thin scar.

This is a face a woman could study forever—if she wasn't too caught up in his body. Because holy shit, he has a *body*. Broad shoulders, tapered hips, and strong legs with muscled calves showing beneath his shorts. Unfortunately, however panty-meltingly hot he is, he's also a brute, and I'm done with men like him. If I have anything to say about it, I'm not touching another MMA superstar—not with a ten-foot pole.

Time to shut this shit down.

"I'm *not* working with you," I tell him, and watch for a change in his expression, but his only reaction is a quick flick of his eyes to the right, where a man in an expensive suit has followed him into my office. "This is *not* a happening thing." I aim this comment at the suit, and he glowers. I don't care. There are some jobs even I won't take, and Adrian wants me to cross a moral line I'm not prepared to.

"Lena," Adrian says in a cautioning tone. "Hold on a moment."

Crossing my arms over my chest, I stare at him, wondering how far he's prepared to push. Considering Jase Rawlins is worth seven or eight figures, I'd hazard a guess that dollar signs are flashing in Adrian's eyes. Too bad. I don't operate that way. Money isn't my driver, and he knows it. So what approach will he take?

————

JASE

Sometimes, I wish it was legal to put someone in a chokehold outside of the cage. Like this uppity image specialist, for instance. Yeah, she may look like a school-boy's wet dream in an ass-hugging pencil skirt and V-necked blouse, but it's obvious from the second she opens her mouth that she's already judged me and found me wanting. Nothing I'm not used to, but it still stings.

Maybe it's the fact my dick has some really great ideas about what he'd like to do with those gorgeous red lips, which are currently set in a sulky pout, or maybe it's her instant dismissal, but I want to rile her. To ruffle up her silky feathers and find out just how mouthy she can get.

I step forward before her boss can intervene, and raise a hand. As expected, everyone falls silent, which only seems to piss the redhead off more. Fuck, we haven't even gotten as far as exchanging names before she's mentally convicted me. That's the shitty part of being in the public spotlight. Everyone thinks they know me. They believe every stupid lie anyone tells.

Well, guess what? This girl doesn't know a goddamn thing.

"Calm down, cutie pie." I love it when her eyes chill to an icy blue, silently threatening to cut my balls off. Yeah, I knew she'd hate the pet name. Considering what she thinks of me, I don't give a crap. "Turns out, I don't want to work with you either." I raise a brow at Nick, my manager, and ask, "Is this really the best you could do?"

The redhead gasps, and I want to check whether she's crossed her arms tighter over her chest, plumping her little tits up, but I resist the urge to look.

"We can go somewhere else," Nick says. "I was told these guys are the best for miracles, but I'm sure we can find someone else just as good."

"Now, wait a minute," the stuffed shirt interjects. I wasn't listening when he introduced himself so I didn't catch his name. "Lena is the best there is. You won't find anyone else."

Finally, I succumb to the desire to glance at her and see how she's taking this. I catch the tail end of an eye-roll, and it makes me soften toward her a little. She's not drinking up the flattery the way some might.

Lena. I try her name out. It suits her. Pretty, bordering on pretentious but not overstepping the mark.

"Whatever puppy dog stunts *Lena*"—I emphasize her

name now that I know it—"wants to pull, they aren't going to do jack." I address Nick. "I still don't get why we're here. Give it a couple of days; Erin will decide she doesn't want to act on her threats, and the hubbub will die down."

Lena's face twists into a sneer. "Die down?" she demands. "The only way this shit-nado is dying down is if someone gets proactive about putting out your fires, and fast. Also, have a little respect for your girlfriend."

"*Ex*-girlfriend."

"Whatever." She says it like the "ex" part doesn't matter. As if Erin and I didn't break up more than two months ago now. "She's not some problem that will disappear if you ignore her. Domestic violence is a serious crime, and you can't just hand-wave it away." Her nose crinkles like she smells something bad. "It disgusts me that you're callous enough to think otherwise."

Callous? Me?

I count to five in my head and remind myself she doesn't know me. Her perception of me is based on what she's seen in the news, and I have to admit, it's damning. It also isn't true, but I don't bother saying that because this woman isn't going to believe me. Stuffing my hands in my pockets, I decide the best way to deal with her is to call her bluff.

"Okay, so you say the problem isn't going away on its own. What did you have in mind to fix it?"

"I… I…" She flounders, and I can't stop the smile that tugs at my lips. She's all bluster and no bite.

"That's what I thought." I turn to leave, but her smarmy boss lays a hand on my arm. When I stare at it, he snaps it back like he's been stung, his cheeks going pale. This guy is even worse than Lena. At least she has the balls to say what she thinks to my face. He's the type who'll pretend to be on my side, but all the while he's secretly fucking terrified of me.

"Wait, wait, wait," he says. "Give me two minutes to speak to Lena in private and talk her around. I promise you won't regret it."

Lena looks like she wants to bash him over the head with a paperweight, and I don't blame her. He's a condescending little shit. "Adrian—" she says.

"My office." He snaps his fingers, like he's ordering a dog to heel. "Now."

They leave, her trailing behind, practically dragging her feet, and Nick gives a low laugh. "Good old Jase. Always charming the ladies."

I jerk a thumb at the door. "Can we go? I've had enough of this."

He sighs, his expression regretful. "I wish we could, but what she said is true. Whether you want to believe it or not, this situation has the potential to derail your career."

"How can it, when I have the championship bout so soon? I'll blow Karson out of the water, and everything will be fine."

Nick ums and ahs. "That's if you don't get arrested before the fight."

"Pfft." I shake my head. "Not gonna happen. Erin is full of hot air."

"She also has a taste for the spotlight, and she'll keep spouting this bullshit as long as the cameras are rolling." Damn, he's right, and he must sense he has the winning hand because he powers on. "Not to mention, you promised Seth you'd take this seriously and do whatever you could not to tarnish the reputation of Crown MMA gym."

Ouch. Low blow. Nick knows I'd go to war for Seth if he asked. My trainer gave me everything. He had faith in me, took a chance on me, and he had no way of knowing I'd pan out to be a good investment. I was just a kid from a poor neighborhood with a mother of a chip on my shoulder and a willingness to shed blood to escape.

"Fine," I concede, not surprising either of us. "I'll hear them out."

But I have a bad feeling about this, and my gut doesn't often lie to me.

Also by A. Rivers

Acknowledgments

My most sincere and heartfelt thank you goes out to the following people:

- My readers, for enjoying my stories and making it possible for me to live a blessed life.
- My husband, the person who makes my world go round.
- My family.
- Renita, Kate, and Donna, for your invaluable work in polishing and fine-tuning this story.
- Maria, for the kickass cover.
- My wonderfully supportive friends, including those in the author community.
- The strong women who fought both against me and by my side during my time in amateur martial arts.

Love you all.
Alexa
XO

About the Author

Alexa (A.) Rivers writes romance with strong heroes and heroines who kick butt and take names. She loves MMA fighters, investigators, military men, bodyguards, and the protective guy next door who isn't afraid to fight the odds for love. She also writes small town romance as Alexa Rivers.

Made in United States
Orlando, FL
18 September 2023

37063772R00067